WORDS OF WISDOM

RUSSIAN FOLK TALES

From
Alexander Afanasiev's
Collection

Illustrated
by A. Kurkin

Raduga Publishers
Moscow

Contents

© Издательство «Советская Россия», 1983 г., иллюстрации
English translation © Raduga Publishers 1987

Н $\frac{4803000000-647}{031(01)-88}$ 051-87

ISBN 5-05-000054-8
ISBN 5-05-001106-X

The Peasant, the Bear and the Fox

A peasant was ploughing his field one day when a bear came up to him and said: "I'm going to kill you, peasant!" "Please don't, *for I'm nothing, bear, if not honest and fair,*" said the peasant. "I'm planting some turnips, and when they're grown I'll give you the tops and leave only the roots for myself." "Very well," said the bear. "But if you trick me, then you'd better not come to the forest for firewood any more or you'll fare badly!" And so saying, he went off into the deep of the forest. The time came for the peasant to dig up the turnips, and as he was doing so the bear came lumbering out of the forest. *Seeing the man, to him he ran.* "Let's divide up the turnips between us now, peasant!" said he. "Let's!" said the peasant. "I'll take the tops to your house if you wish." And he took a whole wagonload of turnip tops to the bear's house. The bear thought that he had been dealt with honestly and was very pleased. And the peasant loaded the turnips on to the wagon and drove to market with them. On the way he met the bear. "Where are you off to, peasant?" the bear asked. "I'm on my way to town to sell these roots," the peasant said. "Let me taste one." The peasant gave him a turnip, and the bear ate it and flew into a temper. "You have tricked me, peasant!" he cried. "Those roots of yours are nice and tasty. Don't you dare come to the forest for firewood any more or I'll kill you!" And the peasant, once he had come back home from town, was much too frightened to venture into the forest. He used up everything there was in the house for firewood, shelves, benches, tubs and barrels, but when nothing more was left he

3

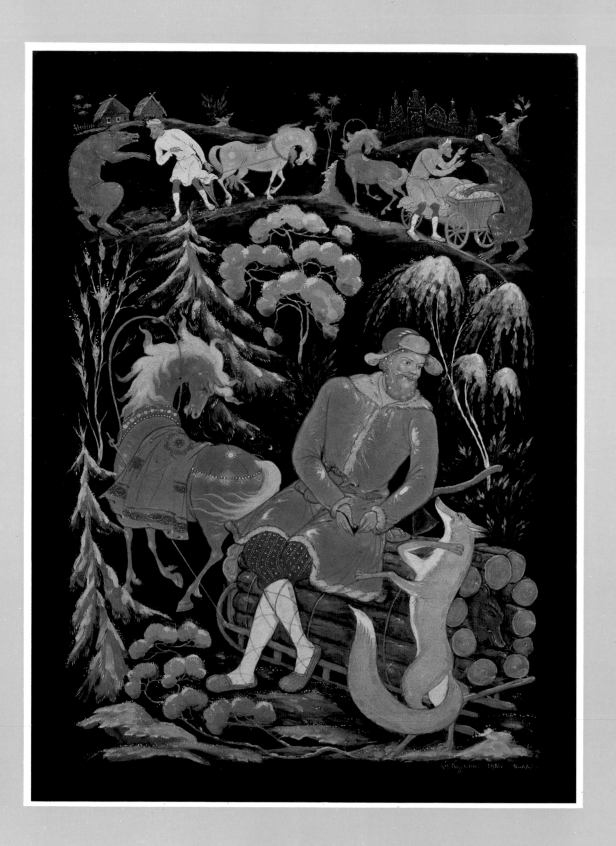

harnessed his horse to a sledge and made for the forest, for what else could he do!

He had the horse go very, very slowly and had just driven into the forest when all of a sudden a fox appeared as if out of thin air and came running toward him. "Why do you drive so slowly, peasant?" asked she. *"It's the bear I fear, for he must be near,* and he promised to kill me," the peasant said. "Chop your wood and have no fear, I'm going to shout and make a lot of noise, and if the bear asks what it all means tell him the hunters are out catching wolves and bears." The peasant began chopping the wood, he looked up, and lo!—he saw the bear come running toward him. *"What's that noise, old man? Tell me if you can!"* he cried. "The hunters are out catching wolves and bears," the peasant said. "Let me get into your sledge, peasant, and when I'm in it, throw some logs over me and tie a rope round them. That'll make the hunters think I'm just another log." The peasant helped the bear into the sledge, tied a rope round him and went at him with the blunt end of his axe. He hit him again and again and did not stop till the bear was quite dead.

By and by the fox came running and asked where the bear was. "Here he is, he's dead!" said the peasant. "Well, now, peasant, don't you think I deserve to be treated to something nice?" "Maybe, maybe, Mistress Fox! Come to my house and I'll do my best for you." The peasant drove off in his sledge, and the fox ran ahead of him, and when he was nearing his house he whistled to his dogs and set them on her. The fox took to her heels, ran into the forest and whisked into her hole. She lay there and called out: "Eyes of mine, eyes of mine, what were you doing as I ran?" "We watched to see that you would not stumble and fall, Mistress Fox!" the eyes replied. "Ears of mine, ears of mine, what were you doing as I ran?" the fox called out again. "We listened hard and tried to hear how far away the dogs were," the ears replied. "What about you, tail of mine, what were you doing as I ran?" the fox called out for the third time. "I dangled between your legs, Mistress Fox, and tried to get you to stumble and fall, so that *though you are clever and live by your wits, the dogs with their teeth would tear you to bits."* "Oh, you no-good tail you!" the fox cried. "Let the dogs eat you up!" And thrusting her tail out of the hole, she shouted: "Come, dogs, eat up my tail!" And the dogs seized the fox by the tail, pulled her out of the hole and made short work of her. It happens often enough that once the tail is lost the head is too.

Translated by Irina Zheleznova

The Crane
and the Heron

An owl, free of care, flew here and flew there, and then happily it lit on a tree. It twirled its tail fast, looked down at the ground and took to the air with never a sound. Now, this is just the little tale before the big tale, and the big tale is still to come.

Once upon a time there lived a crane and a heron who each had a house at the two opposite ends of a swamp. The crane felt very lonely all by himself and decided to get married. "I think I'll go and ask the heron to marry me," said he.

Off he went across the swamp, plunkety-plunk, he waded through it for a whole four miles and then there he was at the heron's doorstep.

"Are you there, Mistress Heron?" he called.

"Yes, I am!" the heron called back.

"Won't you marry me, please?"

"No, Crane, that I won't! Your legs are too long and your coat too short, you are a poor flyer, and you have no food to give me. Go away, Spindly Legs!" So off the crane went, and he got nothing for his pains.

But the heron thought it all over and told herself that it was sad to be without anyone and that she had better marry the crane.

She set out for the crane's house and when she got there, said: "Do please marry me, Crane!"

"No, Mistress Heron, I want none of you!" the crane replied.

6

The heron burst out crying she felt so ashamed, and went home. But after a while the crane thought better of what he had done.

"I shouldn't have refused to marry the heron, life's such a bore when you're all alone," he told himself. "I think I'll go and marry her right now."

He was soon at the heron's doorstep and he said to her: "I have decided to marry you after all, Mistress Heron. Do say yes."

"No, Crane, I don't want you!" said the heron, and she sent him home. But no sooner was he gone than she was sorry she had done so. "It's better to marry the crane than to live all by oneself!" said she. So she went and told the crane that she was ready to marry him. But this time it was he who would not have her. And they've been wooing each other ever since but have never got around to marrying.

Translated by Irina Zheleznova

The Sheep, the Fox
and the Wolf

A sheep once ran away from a peasant, and, coming toward her, she met a fox who asked her where she was going. "Well, now, my dear Mistress Fox," said the sheep, "I was one of a flock owned by a peasant and quite happy for a time, but then life grew quite unbearable. A ram might misbehave, but I was the one to be blamed for it. So that was why I decided to run away and go where the road led."

"It's the same with me," said the fox. "My husband might steal a chicken, but it's me they call thief. Let me come with you!"

On they ran together, and whom should they meet but a wolf.

"Hullo, Mistress Fox, hullo, Mistress Sheep!" said the wolf. "Are you two going far?"

"We are going wherever the road leads," said the fox.

She told him of her plight and that of the sheep, and the wolf said:

"It's exactly the same with me. My wife might kill a lamb, but all the blame is put on me. Let me come with you."

On they went, and the wolf said to the sheep:

"Look here, Mistress Sheep, isn't that my coat you have on?"

And the fox heard him and asked:

"Do you mean it, friend wolf, is it really yours?"

"Yes, it is!"

"Will you swear to it?"

"I will!"

"Will you state it under oath?"

"I will!"

"Come and kiss the cross, then."

Now, the fox had noticed a trap on the path ahead that had been placed there by some peasants, and she led the wolf straight to it.

"Here, kiss this!" said she.

The wolf was foolish enough to believe her. He bent over the trap, and—snap!—was caught fast. And as for the fox and the sheep, they made off at a run, glad to have escaped from the wolf's jaws.

Translated by Irina Zheleznova

Silly Old Grey Wolf

There was once a peasant who lived in a village and had a dog. When the dog was young it guarded the house well, but with old age it grew too weak to bark. The peasant had no use for it, so one day he tied a piece of rope round the dog's neck and led it into the forest. He took the dog up to an aspen tree and was about to hang it, when he saw bitter tears running down its face. He felt sorry for his old dog, tied it to the tree and set off home.

The poor dog was left in the forest and began to cry and curse its lot. Suddenly out of the bushes came a big wolf. It saw the dog and said:

"Good day to you, Hound! I've waited a long time for you to come and see me. You used to chase me away from your house, but now you're in my power, and I can do as I please with you. I'll pay you back now."

"And what do you want to do with me, Grey Wolf?"

"Not much. Just gobble you up, skin, bones and all."

"Stupid Grey Wolf! You're so fat, you don't know what you're doing. Surely you don't fancy scraggy old dog meat after all that tasty beef? Why break your old teeth on an old cur like me? My meat's as tough as leather. I'll tell you what to do. You go and bring me three hundredweight of good horse-flesh, fatten me up a bit, and then do as you please with me."

The wolf did as the dog said. He went off and came back with half a mare for him.

"Here's some meat for you. Eat it up and get fat."

12

And off he went.

The dog took the meat and ate it up. Two days later the stupid wolf came back and said to the dog:

"Well, brother, are you fat now or not?"

"I'm a bit fatter. If you were to bring me a sheep, my meat would get really tasty!"

The wolf agreed to this too, ran off into the field, lay down in a hollow and waited for the shepherd to bring his sheep out to graze. There he came with the flock. The wolf hid behind a bush, picked out a nice fat sheep bigger and fatter than the rest, then leapt out, seized it by the scruff of the neck and dragged it off to the dog.

"Here's a sheep for you. Mind you get fat."

The dog began to get fat. It ate the sheep and began to feel stronger. The wolf came back and asked:

"Well, brother, how are you getting on now?"

"I'm still a bit thin. Now if you were to bring me a wild boar, I'd get as fat as a pig!"

The wolf got a wild boar too, brought it to the dog and said:

"That's my last service. In two days' time I'm coming to get you."

"Very well," thought the dog. "I'll be ready for you."

Two days later the wolf came to the well-fed dog. The dog saw it coming and began to bark loudly.

"Rotten hound," said the grey wolf. "How dare you bark at me!" And he pounced on the dog and tried to tear it to pieces.

But the dog mustered all its strength. It stood on its hind legs and gave the wolf such a welcome, that tufts of its coat went flying. The wolf took to its heels. It raced off, then was about to stop, but as soon as it heard the dog bark, off it ran again.

At last it reached a forest, lay down under a bush and began to lick the wounds it had got from the dog.

"Fancy that rotten dog tricking me like that!" the wolf said to itself. "Now whoever falls into my clutches, won't get away from me now!"

The wolf finished licking its wounds, then went to look for prey. On a hill he saw a large goat. He went up and said:

"Hey, goat! I've come to eat you."

"Oh, no, Grey Wolf! You don't want to break your teeth on me. Stand at the bottom of the hill, open your mouth wide, and I'll run straight into it. Then you can swallow me whole."

The wolf stood at the bottom of the hill and opened his mouth wide. But the crafty goat raced down the hill like the wind and butted the wolf on the forehead so hard that it fell over. And the goat took to its heels.

Some three hours later the wolf recovered with a terrible pain in the head. It started to wonder whether it had eaten the goat or not. It thought and thought, racking its brains.

"If I had eaten the goat, my belly would be nice and full. The goat must have tricked me, the rogue. But I won't let it happen again."

14

So saying the wolf went down to the village, met a sow with her piglets and tried to carry one of the piglets off. But the sow would not let him.

"Daft Porky!" the wolf said to her. "How dare you cross me? I'll tear you to pieces too, and gobble up all your piglets at one go."

But the sow replied:

"I've held my tongue up to now, but now I'll say it. You're a right ninny!"

"Why is that?"

"I'll tell you why. Judge for yourself, how can you eat my piglets? They've only just been born. They must be washed first. You be their godfather, and we'll christen them, the dear little things."

The wolf agreed.

So off they went and came to a big water mill. The sow said to the wolf:

"Go and stand on the other side of the weir, dear godfather, where there is no water, and I will go and dip the piglets in the clear water and hand them to you one by one."

The wolf was as pleased as punch. "Now I'll get my teeth into them alright," it thought. The silly ass went under the bridge, but the sow took the weir lock in her teeth, lifted it up and let out the water. The water came gushing out and swept away the wolf, swirling him round. The sow went home with her piglets, had a good meal, then lay down to sleep on soft straw with her little ones.

When the wolf realised that the sow had tricked it, it clambered onto the bank and set off scouring the forest with an empty belly. At last it was so tormented by hunger that it went down to the village again and saw a dead carcass lying by a barn.

"Good," it thought. "I'll wait until night-time, then eat my fill of that carcass, if there's nothing else."

The wolf had fallen upon bad times, if it was ready to feed upon decaying flesh. But anything was better than to gnash its teeth from hunger and howl its sad lament.

Night came, and the wolf went down to the barn and began to feed on the carcass. But a hunter who had been waiting for it a long time and had prepared a couple of bullets for his old friend, shot it with his gun. The wolf rolled over with the bullets through its head. And that was the end of silly old grey wolf.

Translated by K. M. Cook-Horujy

Mistress Fox
the Confessor

There was once a fox who spent a whole long autumn night stalking game in the forest, but, not having caught anything, felt very hungry. At dawn she came to a village, stole into a hen-house and began trying to climb up on to the perch and seize a hen. Now, this same moment the time came for the rooster to crow, and he flapped his wings, stamped his feet and uttered a loud cry, which so startled the fox that she fell off the perch, took to her heels and lay in a fever for three whole weeks. Soon after this the rooster bethought him of taking a walk in the forest, and there was the fox all ready to spring at him! She hid behind a bush and waited for him to come nearer, but the rooster saw a dry tree, flew up on to one of its branches and sat there very quietly.

The fox found it dull to wait and decided to think of a way of getting the rooster to come down to the ground. She thought and she thought and at last she knew what to do. She came up to the tree and greeted the rooster with a how do you do. "It must have been the devil himself that brought the fox here," thought the rooster. "I wonder what she wants." And the fox, who was very sly, began trying to coax him down off the tree. "I want nothing but your good, Rooster," said she. "I mean to set you on the righteous path and teach you wisdom. Why, Rooster, you have fifty wives, yet you have never once been to confession. Come down off that tree and confess your sins, and I will absolve

you of them and not laugh at you, I promise." The rooster began climbing down off the tree, and lo! —he found himself in the fox's claws. "I'll show you what's what now, Rooster, and make you answer for everything!" cried the fox. "Do you recall all your shameful deeds, you old sinner you? Do you recall how I came to the hen-house on a dark autumn night, not having eaten for three whole days and wanting to take just one little chick for myself, and how you began flapping your wings and stamping your feet?" "It's a wondrous weaver of words you are, Mistress Fox," said the rooster. "You are truly a princess of foxes! Our bishop is soon to hold a feast, and I'm going to ask him to have him make you the church baker. It's the softest of buns you'll bake and the sweetest of mead you'll make, and our fame, yours and mine, will spread throughout." The fox was quite carried away by the rooster's speeches. She let go of him for a moment, and he at once spread his wings and was up in the oak-tree before she could stop him.

Translated by Irina Zheleznova

Mistress Fox
the Midwife

Once upon a time there lived a wolf and a fox who owned a big jar of honey between them. Now, the fox loved sweet things, and as she and the wolf lay in their house she went knock-knock with her tail against the floor. "Isn't someone knocking at the door, Mistress Fox?" the wolf asked. "Oh, that must be one of the neighbours wanting me to help deliver their baby," the fox muttered. "Well, if that's so, you'd better go and do it," the wolf said. At this the fox left the house and made straight for the place where she and the wolf kept the jar of honey. She had her fill of the honey and came back. "Well, has the baby come?" asked the wolf. "Yes, and they've called it Scrape-Top," the fox replied.

Some time passed, and the fox went knock-knock with her tail again. "Isn't that someone knocking at the door, Mistress Fox?" asked the wolf. "That must be one of the neighbours again wanting me to help deliver their baby," said the fox. "Well, then, why don't you go and do it?" The fox left the house and made straight for the place where they kept the jar, and she had so much honey that only a little was left on the bottom. After that she rejoined the wolf who asked her if the baby had come. "Yes, and they've called it Half-Full," said the fox, and she laughed up her sleeve.

On the third day the fox tricked the wolf again in just the same way, and now there was no honey left in the jar, for she had eaten it all. "Has the baby

19

come?" asked the wolf. "Yes, and they've called it Scrape-Bottom," said the fox.

Whether a short time passed or a long nobody knows, but one day the fox pretended to be ill and asked the wolf to fetch her some honey. Off went the wolf to do as she asked, and when he saw the empty jar, he rushed back again. "The jar is empty, Mistress Fox!" he cried. "Someone has eaten all the honey!" "What! Well, it could not have been anyone but you," said the fox. The wolf swore that he had never touched the honey, and the fox said: "Very well, then. Let us lie down in the sun, the honey will melt and seep through the skin, and whichever of us has eaten it will have drops of it showing on his coat."

They lay down in the sun, and the wolf was soon snoring away. As for the fox, she kept awake, and lo! — the honey seeped through her skin and showed on her coat. The fox scraped it off hurriedly and smeared the wolf's coat with it. "Wake up, my friend!" said she, nudging the wolf. "There's honey all over you, and that proves you're the one to have eaten it!" The wolf blinked, and, so foolish was he, begged the fox's forgiveness and said he would never do it again.

So that was a little tale for you, and I'll have some cream and some butter too!

Translated by Irina Zheleznova

A Hen for a Shoe,
a Goose for a Hen

One day, a fox, walking along a forest path, found a bast shoe there. She came to a peasant's house and said:

"Please, my good man, do let me in for the night."

"I can't do that, Foxy, there isn't room enough in here for you," said the peasant.

"Oh, but I don't need much room! I'll curl up on the bench and keep my tail under it."

The peasant let her in, and she said:

"Put this bast shoe of mine in the hen-house."

This he did, and the fox got up in the middle of the night and threw the bast shoe away. Morning came, she asked for her shoe, and the peasant and his wife went to get it but could not find it.

"Your shoe is gone, Foxy!" they said.

"Well, then, give me one of your hens in return for it."

This they did, the fox took the hen, went to the house of another peasant and asked for the hen to be put in the poultry-house, with the geese. Night came, the fox hid the hen and got a goose in return for it in the morning.

She then went to the house of a third peasant and asked to be let in for the night and for her goose to be put in a pen where the sheep were kept. But she

tricked this peasant too, and getting a sheep in return for the goose, made for a fourth house.

There, she asked to be let in for the night and for her sheep to be put in the cowshed. Night came, the fox stole the sheep and hid it and in the morning got the peasant to give her a young bull in return for it.

She killed the hen, the goose, the sheep and the bull, and having hidden the bull's meat, stuffed its skin with straw. The bull now looked like a real bull, and she placed it on the road.

Along came a bear and a wolf, and the fox said to them:

"Go and steal a sledge, and we'll take a ride in it."

The bear and the wolf stole a sledge and yoke too, harnessed the bull to the sledge and climbed into the sledge together with the fox.

The fox began goading on the bull.

"Come, little bull with the side of straw, run, for we want to have a little fun!" she called out. *"The sledge isn't ours, nor is the yoke, so you mustn't tease the village folk!"*

But the bull just stood there and wouldn't move a step.

So then the fox jumped down from the sledge and shouting, "You can stay there, fools, for all I care!" ran away.

The bear and the wolf were very pleased that the bull was all theirs now, and they went at him with their teeth. But when they saw that there was nothing there but skin and straw, they shook their heads and went home.

Translated by Irina Zheleznova

The Goat
With the Peeling Side

Hark, O goat with the peeling side, and a tale I'll spin by the fireside!

There was once a peasant who had a rabbit. One day the peasant went to the field and he saw a goat lying there with the skin half peeled from her side. He felt sorry for her, brought her home with him and put her under a shed. After that he had his dinner and a nap, and, taking the rabbit with him, went out for a look at his vegetable garden. Seeing them, the goat *crept into the house as still as a mouse* and fastened the door with a latch. The rabbit soon felt hungry and ran back to the house. He pushed at the door, but it would not open. "Who's there?" he called. *"Me, the goat with the peeling side, and I warn you, rabbit, to stay outside! If you try to come in, it's badly you'll fare, for I'll butt you hard and your coat I'll tear!"* the goat called back. This made the rabbit very sad, and he walked out of the gate and into the street and began to cry. Now, a wolf happened to be passing by just then, and, seeing the rabbit, he asked him why he was crying. "There's a goat in our house, and she won't leave!" said the rabbit through his tears. "I'll drive her out, don't worry, just come along with me!" said the wolf. They came up to the house, and the wolf asked who was inside. Hearing him, the goat stamped her feet and said: *"Me, the goat with the peeling side, and I warn you, wolf, to stay outside! If you try to come in, it's badly you'll fare, for I'll butt you hard and your coat I'll tear!"*

25

At this the rabbit burst out crying again and stumbled out into the street, and the wolf ran away to the forest. Now, a rooster happened to be passing the house just then, and he saw the rabbit and asked: "Why are you crying, rabbit?" The rabbit told him why, and the rooster said: "Don't worry, I'll drive the goat out, just come along with me!" They made for the house, and in order to frighten the goat, the rabbit called out: *"A rooster is coming, a sword in his hand, and he'll cut off your head if I so command!"* They came up to the door and the rooster asked who was inside. *"Me, the goat with the peeling side, and I warn you, rooster, to stay outside!"* the goat cried. *"If you try to come in, it's badly you'll fare, for I'll butt you hard and your coat I'll tear!"*

The rabbit burst into tears again and stumbled out into the street, and lo! — a bee came flying up to him. Round and round it flew and it asked the rabbit why he was crying and if anyone had treated him badly. The rabbit told the bee about the goat, and the bee flew to the house. "Who is inside this house?" it asked. And the goat answered it in just the same way she had the others. This made the bee very angry and it went flying round and round the house, buzzing loudly as it did so. Then, seeing a little hole in the wall, it crawled inside through it and stung the goat hard in her peeling side. *The side swelled, the goat yelled,* and away she ran out of the door and through the gate. And the rabbit whisked into the hut. *He drank some water and ate lots of food, and went to bed, feeling very good. When he wakes up, which he'll do in time, I'll spin a long tale and make up a rhyme.*

Translated by Irina Zheleznova

The Bubble, the Straw and the Bast Shoe

Once upon a time there lived a bubble, a straw and a bast shoe. The three of them went to the forest for firewood, and, coming to a stream, stopped, for they did not know how to cross it. "Let me and the straw get on your back, bubble, and you'll swim across," said the bast shoe. "No, bast shoe, let the straw stretch itself from bank to bank, and you and me will walk across." The straw did as it was told, but when the bast shoe started walking across it, the straw broke, and both of them fell into the water. Seeing them, the bubble began to laugh, and it laughed so hard that it burst and nothing was left of it!

Translated by Irina Zheleznova

Father Frost

There was once a woman who had a daughter of her own and a step-daughter too. No matter what her own daughter did, she petted and kissed her and said that she was a good and a clever girl. But the stepdaughter, try hard as she would, could not please her, she found fault with her at every step, and *not a day went by but she made her cry.* Now, if the truth be told, the stepdaughter was a good girl, as good as gold, and she would have been quite happy with anyone save her stepmother.

What was there to do? A wind howls loud and then it drops, but there is no quieting an old dame once she is roused. And so it was with the stepmother who made up her mind to drive her stepdaughter out of the house.

"Take her away, old man," said she to her husband, "take her away as far as you want, just so my eyes don't see her and my ears don't hear her. Take her to the open field, into the biting frost!"

The old man wept and sorrowed, but he put his daughter in a sledge, and he did not even cover her with a horse cloth, as he meant to, for fear of his wife. Off he drove with her to the open field where he dumped her on to a snowdrift, made the sign of the cross over her, and, not wanting to watch her die, drove away.

The poor girl sat there shivering and saying her prayers, and lo and behold!

—there was Father Frost coming toward her, leaping and dancing as he did so.

"*I am Father Frost, my pretty lass, and they call me Red Nose wherever I pass!*" he cried. "Welcome, Father Frost!" said the girl. "It must have been God himself who sent you here after me, sinner that I am." Father Frost had meant to freeze the girl to death, but he liked her for the clever words she spoke and took pity on her. He threw her his warm coat, and she put it on and sat there, her feet tucked under her. Father Frost went away, but he was soon back again, and *he leapt and danced and at the girl glanced. "I am Father Frost, my pretty lass, and they call me Red Nose wherever I pass!*" he called. "Welcome, Father Frost!" said the girl. "It must have been God himself who sent you here after me, sinner that I am." But Father Frost had not come to freeze the girl but to bring her gifts. He had with him a large chest full of many fine things, and this he now gave to her. The girl sat down on the chest, and she looked very pretty and very happy too. Father Frost went away again, but he was back very soon for the third time, and *he leapt and danced and at the girl glanced.* The girl welcomed him with a kind and a gentle word, and he made her a gift of a dress sewn with gold and silver. She put the dress on, *and there never was one as fair as she nor dressed in such fancy finery*!

Meanwhile, her stepmother had prepared a funeral feast in her memory and baked a plateful of pancakes. "Go to the field, husband, and bring back your daughter to be buried here," said she. The old man set out for the field, and the stepmother's little dog, who was hiding under the table, said: "Bow-wow! *The old man's daughter comes a rich bride and fair, but the old woman's daughter will marry ne'er!*" "Shut your mouth, you fool of a dog you!" said the old woman. "Here, eat a pancake and say: '*The old woman's daughter will be wooed and won, but the old man's daughter is dead and gone!*' " The dog ate the pancake, but still it said: "*The old man's daughter comes a rich bride and fair, but the old woman's daughter will marry ne'er!*" The old woman threw more pancakes to the dog and she beat it for good measure, and still the dog went on to say what it had before: "*The old man's daughter comes a rich bride and fair, but the old woman's daughter will marry ne'er!*"

Just then the gate creaked, the door flew open, and a great, heavy chest was carried in. And behind it came the old man's daughter, dazzling in her garb of silver and gold. The old woman dropped her hands in dismay. "Come, old man, hurry and harness some fresh horses and take my daughter to the selfsame place in the selfsame field!" cried she. The old man did as she bade and left the girl in the field, and by and by Father Frost came there. But though *he leapt and danced and at the girl glanced,* she never said a kind word to him, and this so angered him that he gripped her with all his might and froze her to death. "Come, old man, it's time for you to bring back my daughter," said the stepmother. "You must harness our fastest horses, and mind that you do not overturn

the sledge or let the chest fall!" Off the old man drove, and the dog hiding under the table said: "Bow-wow! *The old man's daughter will soon be wed, but the old woman's daughter is cold and dead!*" "You speak wrong, dog!" the old woman said. "Here's a pie for you. Come now, say: 'The old woman's daughter comes a rich bride and fair!' "

Just then the gate flew open, and out the old woman ran to meet her daughter. But her daughter lay in the sledge, dead, and though she cried and wept over her it was all too late.

Translated by Irina Zheleznova

Tiny

There once lived an old man and an old woman. One day, the old woman decided to bake some pies, and as she was chopping up the cabbage for the filling she accidentally sliced her little finger off with the knife. She did not stop to think and flung away the finger, but no sooner had she done so than she heard someone saying to her from behind the stove:

"Please, Mother, take me out of here!"

This made her step back in surprise, but she crossed herself and asked:

"And who may you be?"

"I am your little son, Mother. Your little finger turned into a boy, and I am he."

The old woman picked the boy up—he was so tiny that you could hardly see him when he stood on the floor—and she called him Tiny.

"Where is my father?" Tiny asked.

"In the field."

"I think I'll go and help him plough."

"Do that, child."

Tiny came to the field, and, seeing the old man, called out:

"All power to your elbow, Father!"

The old man glanced about him.

"This is strange indeed!" said he. "I can hear someone's voice, but I don't see anyone. Who is it that has just spoken to me?"

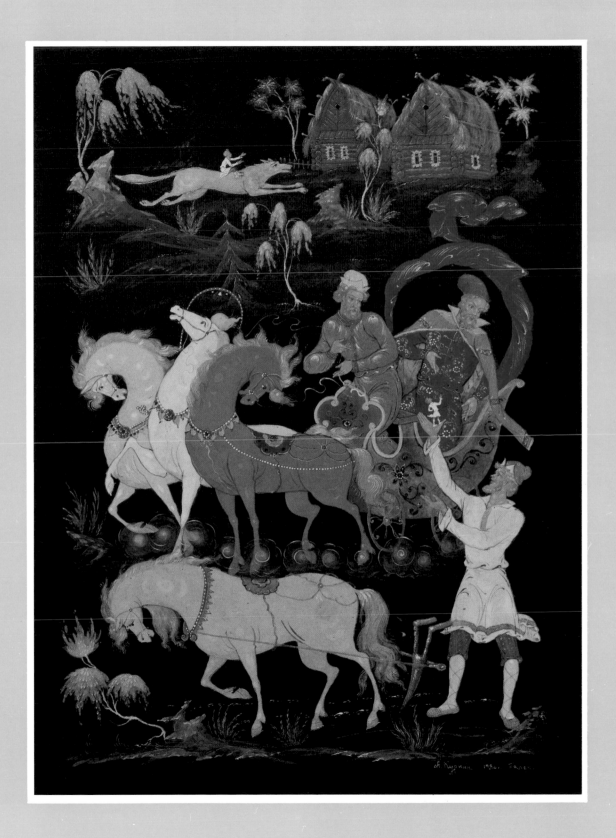

"Me, your little son, Father."

"But I have no children, never had any."

"I was only born a little while ago. Mother was chopping cabbage for her pies, and she sliced off her little finger with the knife. She threw the finger behind the stove, and lo!—there I was in its place. She called me Tiny, and I am here to help you plough. You sit down and rest, Father, and have a bite to eat."

The old man was overjoyed. He sat down and unwrapped his food, and Tiny climbed into the horse's ear and began to plough, but not before he had said to his father:

"If anyone offers to buy me, don't hesitate but sell me to him. Never fear—nothing will happen to me, I'll come right back."

Now, a landlord was driving past just then and when he saw the horse ploughing all by itself he was quite taken aback.

"Why, if that isn't a horse ploughing all by itself!" said he. "Never has anyone seen the like of this!"

"What's come over you—you must be blind!" the old man said. "That is not the horse but my son ploughing."

"Your son? Where is he, then?"

"In the horse's ear."

"Sell him to me."

"I can't do that! He is my old woman's and mine only joy in life."

"Come, now, old man, I will pay you well!"

"Give me a thousand roubles, and he's yours!"

"Isn't that asking too much?"

"You can see for yourself: *the boy is small, but by no means dumb; he's quick on his feet and as brave as they come.*"

The landlord paid out the thousand roubles, put Tiny in his pocket and drove home, but the little boy peed in his pocket, made a hole in it and slipped out.

He decided to walk along the road, he walked and he walked, and it was night before he knew it. He lay down under a blade of grass by the wayside and was about to go to sleep when he saw three men, three robbers, walking past.

"Hullo there, my fine fellows!" Tiny called out.

"Hullo, little man!"

"Where are you going?"

"To the priest's house."

"What for?"

"To steal his bullocks."

"Take me with you!"

"What good will you be to us? We need someone big and strong, someone who need use his fists but once to bring down any who try to stop him!"

"I may be of use to you all the same. I'll crawl under the gate and open it for you."

"A good idea! Come along, then."

Tiny joined them, and the four of them soon came to the priest's house. They stopped by the gate, and Tiny crawled under it and opened it.

"Come into the yard and wait for me, brothers," he said, "and I'll get into the barn, pick the best of the bullocks and lead him out to you."

"All right, go ahead and do it!"

Tiny did not wait to be told a second time.

He got into the barn and called as loud as he could:

"Which bullock do you want—the brown or the black one?"

"Don't make so much noise!" the robbers called back. "Either one will do."

Tiny led the finest of the bullocks out to them, and the robbers drove him to the forest, slaughtered and skinned him and began dividing up the meat.

"I'll take the tripe for myself, brothers, it'll do for me," said Tiny.

He took the tripe, curled up under it where no one could see him and went to sleep, and the robbers divided the meat and went home.

All of a sudden a hungry wolf came running up, and he swallowed all of the tripe and Tiny, who was fast asleep, with it.

There sat Tiny in the wolf's stomach, safe and sound, and he had not a care in the world! But the wolf was in a bad way. He would see a flock of sheep grazing in a field and the shepherd sleeping nearby, but no sooner would he steal up close in order to carry off one of them than Tiny would call out:

"*Shepherd, shepherd, do not sleep, the wolf will carry off your sheep!*"

At this the shepherd would wake, fall on the wolf with a cudgel and set the dogs on him, the dogs would worry him half to death and send tufts of his fur flying, and he would only get away by the skin of his teeth!

And as this happened time and again, the wolf went hungry and was soon all skin and bones.

"Please, whoever you are, climb out of my stomach!" he begged.

"Take me home to my mother and father, and I will!" Tiny said.

The wolf made straight for the village and the old man's house, he ran inside, and Tiny crawled out of his stomach and cried:

"Hurry, Mother, hurry, Father, beat the wolf black and blue!"

The old man seized a stick, and the old woman another, and they went at the wolf, killed and skinned him and made a warm coat for Tiny out of the skin. And after that they all lived happily together till it was time for them to die.

Translated by Irina Zheleznova

Wee Little Havroshechka

There are good people in the world and there are bad ones too. There are also some who fear neither God nor man and are shameless in their wickedness. And it was with just such as these that Wee Little Havroshechka had the bad luck to fall in. She had been left an orphan at an early age, and these people took her in and brought her up only to make her work beyond her strength. *In the house till dark she was made to stay, and they forced her to toil all the long day.* She fetched and carried and scrubbed the floor and had to do many other things besides.

Now, her mistress had three grown daughters, the eldest of whom was called One-Eye, the middle one, Two-Eyes, and the youngest, Three-Eyes. All the three sisters did was sit by the gate all day and watch what went on in the street, while Wee Little Havroshechka spun and wove and sewed for them. And she never heard a kind word in return. And that was what hurt most—there was always someone to hit or push her, but never anyone to smile at her or make her feel welcome.

Sometimes Wee Little Havroshechka would go out into the field, put her arms round the neck of her brindled cow and pour out all her sorrows to her. "Brindled, my dear," she would say, "*they beat and they scold me, I know not why, and tell me that I must never cry.* And yet I am to have five poods of flax spun, woven, bleached and rolled by tomorrow." And the cow would say in reply: "My bonny lass, you have only to climb into one of my ears and out of

38

the other, and it will all be done for you." And just as Brindled said, so it was. Wee Little Havroshechka would climb into one of the cow's ears and out of the other, and lo!—there lay the cloth all woven and bleached and rolled. Wee Little Havroshechka would then take the rolls of cloth to her mistress who would look at them and grunt and put them away in a chest and give Wee Little Havroshechka even more work to do. And Wee Little Havroshechka would go to Brindled, climb into one of her ears and out of the other and take the ready cloth to her mistress again.

This made the old woman wonder, and one day she called One-Eye and said to her: "My good child, my bonny child, go and see who helps the orphan with her work. Find out who spins the yarn and weaves the cloth and rolls it. That's something you can surely do." One-Eye followed Wee Little Havroshechka into the woods and out to the field, but she forgot what her mother had told her to do. She lay down on the grass and basked in the sun, and Wee Little Havroshechka murmured: "Sleep, little eye, sleep!" One-Eye shut her eye and went to sleep. While she slept, Brindled wove, bleached and rolled the cloth. The old woman learnt nothing, so she sent Two-Eyes on the same errand. But Two-Eyes lay down on the grass and basked in the sun and forgot what her mother had told her to do. And Wee Little Havroshechka murmured: "Sleep, little eye! Sleep, the other little eye!" Two-Eyes dozed off, and while she slept, Brindled wove, bleached and rolled the cloth.

The old woman was very angry, and on the following day she bade Three-Eyes go with Wee Little Havroshechka to whom she gave more work to do than ever. Like her two elder sisters, Three-Eyes played and skipped about in the sun until she was so tired that she lay down on the grass. And Wee Little Havroshechka sang out: "Sleep, little eye! Sleep, the other little eye!" But she forgot all about the third eye. Two of Three-Eyes' eyes slept, but the third looked on and saw everything: it saw Wee Little Havroshechka climb into one of Brindled's ears and out of the other and pick up the ready cloth. Three-Eyes told her mother of all that she had seen, and the old woman, who was as pleased as pleased can be, said to her husband on the very next day: "Go and slaughter the brindled cow." The old man tried to reason with her. "Have you lost your wits, wife?" said he. "The cow is a good cow and still young!" But she would not listen to him and demanded that he do as he was told. The old man began sharpening his knife, and seeing him, Wee Little Havroshechka ran to the field. "Brindled, my dear, they want to kill you!" she cried. "Do not grieve, my bonny lass, and do as I tell you," said the cow. "Once I am dead, take my bones, tie them up in a kerchief, bury them in the garden and water them every day. And mind, do not eat of my flesh and never forget me."

Wee Little Havroshechka did as Brindled had told her. She went hungry, but would not touch the meat, and she buried the bones in the garden and watered them every day. After a while an apple-tree grew up out of them, and a wonderful tree it was! Its apples were round and juicy, its swaying boughs were of silver and its rustling leaves were of gold. Whoever drove by would stop to look, and whoever came near marvelled.

One day One-Eye, Two-Eyes and Three-Eyes were out walking in the garden. And who should chance to come riding by just then but a young man who was young and handsome, and rich besides. Seeing the apples, he said to the girls teasingly: "Fair maidens! *Her will I marry amongst you three who brings me an apple from yonder tree.*" And the sisters rushed to the apple-tree, each trying to get ahead of the others. But the apples, which had been hanging very low and seemed within easy reach, now swung up high in the air above the sisters' heads. The sisters tried to knock them down, but the leaves came down in a shower and blinded them. They tried to pluck the apples, but the boughs caught in their braids and unplaited them. Struggle as they would, they could not reach the apples and only scratched their hands. Then Wee Little Havroshechka walked up to the tree, and the boughs bent low and the apples came down into her hands. The handsome young stranger married her, and from that day on *she knew no woe, shed never a tear and prospered the more from year to year.*

Translated by Irina Zheleznova

The Crystal Mountain

In a certain kingdom, in a certain realm there was once a king who had three sons. One day the sons said to him: "Give us your blessing, Father, for we want to go hunting." The king blessed them, and away they rode in three different directions. The youngest son, who was named Prince Ivan, rode on and on for a long time, but he lost his way and found himself in a forest glade where lay a dead horse. A great many beasts, birds and snakes were gathered round it, and, seeing the prince, a falcon rose into the air and lighted on his shoulder. "Do please divide this horse among us, Prince Ivan," said he. "It has been lying here for thirty-three years, but we do not know how to do it and only keep arguing." The prince did as he was asked. He got off his trusty steed and began dividing up the horse. To the beasts of prey he gave its bones, to the birds, its flesh, to the snakes, its skin, and to the ants, its head. "Many thanks to you, Prince Ivan!" said the falcon. "You have done us a great service, and now here is your reward: any time you wish you can turn into either a falcon or an ant."

Prince Ivan struck the damp earth, turned into a falcon, and, soaring to the sky, made for the thrice-ten realm which was famed for the crystal mountain that had formed on top of it. He flew straight to the palace, got back his proper shape and asked of the palace guards whether the king would let him take up service with him. "Why would he refuse to take on a fine young man like you?" they said. The prince took up service with the king, and he lived in the palace for a week and another and a third. One day the princess saw him, and she begged her father to let her ride with him to the crystal mountain. To this the king gave his permission, and the prince and princess got on their trusty steeds and set off on their way. They were nearing the mountain when, as if out of thin air, a golden goat appeared before them. The prince put his horse into a gallop and rode after it. He rode and he rode for a long time, but the goat vanished from sight, and when he turned round and came back he saw that the princess too was gone! What was he to do? How could he dare show himself to the king?

The prince thought it over and decided to pass himself off as a very old man. He so disguised himself that no one could have possibly known him, and, coming to the palace, asked the king to let him tend his herd. "Very well," said the king. "I don't mind. But remember this: if you meet with a three-headed dragon, you must give him three cows; if with a six-headed dragon, you must give him six cows; and if with a twelve-headed dragon, you must give him twelve cows." Prince Ivan drove his herd over the hills and dales and had left them behind him when all of a sudden who should come flying toward him but a three-headed dragon. "Ah, Prince Ivan, you do what ill befits you!" said he. "A brave lad like you should be fighting, and here you are tending cattle. Come, now, give me three of your cows." "Aren't you asking for too much?" said the prince. "*I only eat a duck a day, and you want three cows, as I heard you say.* Well, not one will you get!" The dragon flew into a temper and instead of three cows seized twice as many. But the prince would not be thwarted. He turned himself into a falcon, smote off the dragon's three heads and drove his herd home. "Did the three-headed dragon come for his three cows, old man?" the king asked. "He came for them, yes, Your Majesty, but he got nothing for his trouble," said Prince Ivan.

On the following day Prince Ivan again drove his herd over the hills and dales, and lo!—a six-headed dragon came flying towards him from the lakeside where he lived and demanded six cows of him. "You glutton you!" Prince Ivan cried. "*I only eat a duck a day, and you want six cows, as I heard you say.* Well, not one will you get!" The dragon flew into a temper and seized twelve cows instead of six, but Prince Ivan turned himself into a falcon, and, falling on the dragon, smote off all six of his heads. After that he drove the herd home. "Did the six-headed dragon come for his six cows, old man, and did you give them to him?" the king asked. "He came for them, yes, but he got nothing for his troubles!" Prince Ivan said. Night came, and he changed himself into an ant and crept into the crystal mountain through a small crack in its side. And whom should he see there but the princess, the very one he had despaired of ever seeing again. "Greetings to you, Princess," said Prince Ivan. "How ever did you get here?" "I was seized and brought here by the twelve-headed dragon who lives by the side of the lake," said the princess. "There is a chest hid in the dragon's body, in that chest there is a hare, in the hare a duck, in the duck an egg, and in the egg a seed. If you kill the dragon and get the seed out from inside him, you will be able to melt down the crystal mountain and free me from captivity."

Prince Ivan crawled out of the mountain, donned his shepherd's dress and drove his herd to pasture, and lo!—who should come flying toward him but the twelve-headed dragon. "Ah, Prince Ivan, you do what ill befits you," said the

dragon. "A brave lad like you should be out fighting, and here you are herding cattle. Come, count off twelve cows and give them to me!" "That's far too many!" said Prince Ivan. "*Why, I only eat a duck a day, and you want twelve cows, as I heard you say!*" They began to fight, and whether they fought for a short or a long time nobody knows, but Prince Ivan killed the twelve-headed dragon and cut up his body. He found a chest inside it, a hare in the chest, a duck in the hare, an egg in the duck, and a seed in the egg. He set fire to the seed and held it close to the crystal mountain, and lo!—the crystal mountain began to melt and soon melted quite away. Prince Ivan led out the princess and took her to her father, and so overjoyed was the king that he offered her to the prince in marriage. They were wed there and then, and a feast was held to celebrate the wedding. I was at the feast too, *I drank ale and I drank wine, but it all ran down this beard of mine* and not a drop got into my mouth.

Translated by Irina Zheleznova

Fearless Frolka

There was once a king who had three daughters more beautiful than tale can tell or pen describe. In the evening they liked to take a walk in their garden, which was a fine big one. And Dragon Chernomor also took to flying there.

One day the king's daughters lingered late in the garden, looking at the flowers. Suddenly out of nowhere down swooped Dragon Chernomor and carried them off on his fiery wings.

The king waited and waited for his daughters to return. He sent maidservants to look for them in the garden, but all in vain. They could not find the princesses.

Next morning the king raised the alarm and a large crowd gathered. Then the king said to them:

"He who finds my daughters shall have as much gold as he desires."

Three stalwarts were chosen—a soldier fond of his cups, Fearless Frolka and Yeryoma. They made a bargain with the king and went off to look for the princesses.

On and on they walked until they came to a dense forest. No sooner had they entered it, than began to feel drowsy. Fearless Frolka took his snuff-box out of his pocket, tapped it, opened it and pushed a pinch of snuff up his nostril. Then he cried:

"Come on, lads, we mustn't drop off! Let's be on our way!"

So on they plodded, until at last they came to a huge palace where a five-headed dragon lived. They knocked long at the gate, but no one came. Then Fearless Frolka pushed the soldier and Yeryoma aside.

"Let me have a go, lads!"

He took a pinch of snuff and rammed the gate so hard that he smashed it to pieces.

They went into the courtyard, sat down in a circle and were about to eat what the good Lord had sent them, when out of the palace came a maid, fair as fair can be, and said:

"Why have you come here, my good men? A terrible dragon lives here, and he will gobble you up! You're lucky he isn't at home now."

To which Frolka replied:

"We'll gobble him up ourselves!"

No sooner were the words out of his mouth, than up flew the dragon, roaring loudly.

"Who has been destroying my kingdom? Does anyone dare to be my foe? I do have one foe, but he is so far away that the raven shall not bear his bones here."

"The raven will not bear me here," said Frolka. "But my trusty steed will!"

Hearing these words, the dragon asked:

"Have you come to make peace or battle?"

"I've come not to make peace," replied Frolka, "but to make battle."

Then they charged at each other in mortal combat, and Frolka cut off the dragon's five heads at one fell swoop, placed them under a rock and buried the body in the ground. The fair maid was overjoyed and said to the stalwart youths:

"Take me with you, my good men."

"Who is your father?" they asked.

She replied that she was the king's daughter. Frolka told her of their errand, and they got on well. The princess took them into the palace, gave them food and drink, and begged them to free her other sisters as well.

"That is why we have been sent!" said Frolka.

The princess told them where her sisters were living.

"My middle sister's fate was even worse than mine. She is living with a seven-headed dragon."

"Never fear!" said Frolka. "We'll manage him alright. It's only the twelve-headed dragon that will take me a bit more time."

They bade her farewell and went on their way.

Then they came to the palace where the middle sister was held captive. The palace was a huge one surrounded by high iron railings. They went up and found the gate. Frolka hammered on the gate with all his might and it swung open. They went into the courtyard and again sat down to have a bite to eat.

Suddenly up flew the seven-headed dragon.

"I smell the blood of a Russian!" he roared. "Oh, it's you, Frolka. What have you come for?"

"I'll show you what!" Frolka replied. He struck the dragon, cut off all

48

seven heads in one fell swoop, put them under a rock and buried the body in the ground.

Then they went into the palace. They looked in one room, then in another, and in the fourth they saw the middle princess sitting on a sofa. When they told her how and why they had come, she was overjoyed, gave them food and drink and begged them to save her youngest sister from the twelve-headed dragon. Frolka said:

"To be sure. That's what we were sent for! Only my blood runs cold! But the good Lord will help us! Bring us another goblet each."

They drank them down and went on their way. At last they came to a steep gorge. On the other side of the gorge stood two huge posts instead of a gate, and chained to the posts were two terrible lions who roared so loudly that Frolka alone stood firm on his feet, while his companions fell to the ground in terror. Frolka said to them:

"I have seen more fearsome things than this and not flinched. Follow me!"

So on they went.

Suddenly out of the palace came an old man of about seventy or so. Seeing them, he came up and said:

"Where are you going, my good men?"

"Into the palace," Frolka replied.

"Then you go to certain death, my lads, for in this palace lives a twelve-headed dragon. He is not at home now, or he would have gobbled you up already!"

"It's him we're looking for!"

"In that case come with me," the old man said. "I will take you there."

The old man went up to the lions and began to stroke them, while Frolka and his companions slipped into the courtyard.

They entered the palace, and the old man took them to the room where the princess lived. When she saw them, she jumped up quickly from the bed and asked them who they were and why they had come. They told her all. The princess gave them food and drink, and herself began to get ready.

No sooner had they left the palace, than they saw the dragon a mile off flying towards them. The princess fled back into the palace, but Frolka and his companions advanced to give battle. At first the dragon got the better of them, but Frolka was a canny lad. He slew the dragon, cut off all his twelve heads and threw them into the gorge.

Then they went into the palace and made merry. After that they collected the other princesses and all arrived back in their kingdom together.

The king was beside himself with joy. He unlocked his coffers and said:

"Here, my faithful servants, take as much money as you like for your work."

Now Frolka was a clever lad. He fetched his big fur cap. The soldier brought his knapsack, and Yeryoma brought an egg basket. Frolka was the first to pour the silver into his cap. He poured so much that it tore, and the silver fell out and vanished into the mud. Then he began to pour again and this time the coins fell out of the cap.

"Well, I never!" said Frolka. "It looks like I'm going to get all the king's silver."

"Then what'll be left for us?" asked his companions.

"Never fear, the king has money enough for you too!"

Then Yeryoma filled his basket with silver, while there was still some left, and the soldier filled his knapsack, and off they went home. But Frolka stayed by the king's coffers with his cap, and is still there to this day pouring away. When he's filled it, I'll tell you the rest of the tale. But now I have neither the strength nor the inclination.

Translated by K. M. Cook-Horujy

Ivan the Bull's Son

In a certain tsardom, in a certain realm there lived a tsar and a tsarina who had no children. One day they began praying to God to give them a child for them to feast their eyes on while they were young and to care for them in their old age, and, *their prayers said, went to bed.*

They fell fast asleep, and both of them saw the same dream. They dreamt that in the lake near the palace, and a quiet little lake it was, there lived a gold-scaled ruff, and if the tsarina were to eat it she would at once find herself with child.

The tsar and tsarina woke, they called their maids and women and told them what they had seen in their dream. And the maids and women heard them out, and, after having thought it over, said that whatever one sees in one's dream is bound to happen in real life.

So the tsar had some fishermen summoned and bade them catch the gold-scaled ruff.

The fishermen came to the lake at daybreak, cast their net and had the good luck to catch the gold-scaled ruff at the first try. They took him out of the net and brought him to the palace, and, seeing them, the tsarina could not keep her seat. Up she jumped, snatched the ruff out of their hands and gave them a bag of money. *And the reward was well deserved, for well had they their sovereigns served!* The tsarina then called her favourite cook and gave the ruff to her.

51

"Here," says she. "Cook the ruff for my dinner and see that none save you touches it."

The cook cleaned and washed the ruff, cooked it and took the pail with the slops out into the yard. The tsarina ate the fish, the cook ate the leavings, and a cow that was out in the yard lapped up the slops, and all three of them became pregnant at one and the same time and gave birth at one and the same time too.

The tsarina was delivered of a son whom she named Prince Ivan, the cook, of a son who went by the name of Ivan the Cook's Son, and the cow, of a son who was called Ivan the Bull's Son.

The three grew not by the day but by the hour, as fast as dough rises when the yeast is good, and they all looked alike, so that none could say which of them was the tsar's son, which the cook's, and which the cow's. It was only by the way they behaved when they came back from a dance or a fête that they could be told apart at all, for Prince Ivan would call for a fresh shirt, the cook's son for a hearty meal, and Ivan the Bull's Son would go straight to bed.

When the three were in their tenth year they came to the tsar and said:

"Please, O tsar, our father, have an iron stick fifty poods in weight made for us."

The tsar ordered his blacksmiths to forge an iron stick weighing fifty poods, and the blacksmiths set to work and had it ready by the end of the week. So heavy was the stick that none could so much as lift it, but Prince Ivan, Ivan the Cook's Son and Ivan the Bull's Son could twirl it between their fingers as easily as though it was a goose quill.

The three of them stepped out into the palace courtyard, and Prince Ivan said:

"Let us test our strength, brothers, and he who proves to be the strongest shall be as an elder brother to us, and we shall do as he says."

"Agreed," said Ivan the Bull's Son. "Take the stick and beat us over the shoulders with it."

Prince Ivan took the iron stick, struck Ivan the Cook's Son and Ivan the Bull's Son with it and drove them knee-deep into the ground. Then Ivan the Cook's Son took the stick, he struck Prince Ivan and Ivan the Bull's Son with it, and he drove them chest-deep into the ground. But when the turn of Ivan the Bull's Son came to wield the stick, he drove his two brothers neck-deep into the ground.

"Let us test our strength once again," Prince Ivan said. "Let us each throw the stick into the air, and he who throws it higher than the other two shall be as an elder brother to us, and we shall do as he says."

"Well, then, you be the first to throw it!"

Prince Ivan hurled the stick into the air, and it was back on the ground again before a quarter of an hour had passed. Ivan the Cook's Son hurled the stick into the air, and it fell to the ground in half an hour. But when came the turn of Ivan the Bull's Son, he hurled the stick so high that it only came flying back when a whole hour had passed.

"You have proved your worth and shall be as an elder brother to us, and we shall do as you say, Ivan the Bull's Son," said his brothers.

This settled, they went for a walk in the garden and soon came upon a huge stone lying on the ground before them.

"Isn't that stone big! I wonder if it can be lifted," Prince Ivan said. He took hold of the stone, but try hard as he would he could not so much as move it.

Ivan the Cook's Son was the next to take hold of the stone, but all he could do was move it a little.

"Pooh! Not equal to it, you two!" Ivan the Bull's Son said. "Now let me try and see if I can lift it."

He came up to the stone and gave it a push with his foot, and the stone gave out a booming sound and went rolling to the other end of the garden, felling many trees as it rolled. And where the stone had been now gaped a hole in the ground, a kind of deep cellar in which stood three giant steeds, while on the cellar walls hung harness of a kind used by warriors. Here was something for the three brothers—something that could help them show their prowess!

Nor did they tarry but at once went to see the tsar.

"Please, O tsar, our father," they said, "give us your blessing. For we wish to go to faraway lands to take a look at the folk who live there and to show ourselves to them!"

The tsar gave them his blessing and some money too, they bade him goodbye, mounted the three giant steeds and set out on their way.

On they rode across hills and dales, along rocky roads and weed-grown trails, and they came to a dark forest where, *turning round and round without a sound,* stood a hut on chicken feet, on sheep horns.

"Please, hut, stand as once you stood, with your face to us and your back to the wood," said they. *"We're all done in and dead on our feet, and we want to ask for a bite to eat."*

The hut turned and faced them, the three brothers stepped inside, and there before them, lying on a stone ledge, *was Baba-Yaga the Leg of Stone, a very, very old and wicked crone. And so twisted was she that she seemed to be kneeling, for her mouth reached the floor and her nose touched the ceiling.*

"Fee-fo-fum! Russian blood! I never smelt it before, no, nor even heard of it. *But now it's here and asking to be put on a spoon and eaten by me."*

"Enough, old one! *Don't you scold and don't you drool, but get off the stove and sit on a stool,"* said Ivan the Bull's Son. "Ask us where we are bound, and I'll answer you politely."

And Baba-Yaga at once climbed down from the stove and came up to Ivan the Bull's Son. *She no longer looked grim and she bowed to him.*

"Good morrow to you, Ivan the Bull's Son!" said she. *"I'm right glad to see you, my lad.* Whither bound? For what far land?"

"We are on our way to the Currant River, Grandma, which is spanned by the Cranberry Bridge. I hear that that is where the three Chudo-Yudos live."

"Good for you! You're doing right to be going there. *Those dragons are villains, every one, and 'tis much evil they have done.* They have overrun all the neighbouring realms, laid them waste and taken the people captive."

The three brothers spent the night in Baba-Yaga's house and as soon as it

was morning set out on their way again. They came to the Currant River, and they saw that human bones lay piled knee-high on the shore. A hut stood there, they came inside, and, seeing that it was empty, decided to put up in it.

Evening came, and Ivan the Bull's Son said:

"We find ourselves in a strange land, brothers, and we must beware of danger. Let us take turns keeping watch."

They cast lots then and there, and the lot fell upon Prince Ivan to keep watch the first night, Ivan the Cook's Son, the second night, and Ivan the Bull's Son, the third night.

Off went Prince Ivan to keep watch, but instead of doing so he lay down behind some bushes and fell fast asleep. Now, Ivan the Bull's Son felt he could not put much trust in him, and no sooner was it midnight than he was up and on his feet, and, taking his sword and shield with him, stepped outside and stationed himself under the Cranberry Bridge.

All of a sudden waves rose on the river, the eagles sitting on the tops of the oak-trees uttered a shrill cry, and Chudo-Yudo the Dragon, he of the six heads, came riding up. But his horse stumbled under him, the black raven perching on his shoulder shook his wings, and the hunting dog that ran behind him bristled.

Said Chudo-Yudo the Dragon, he of the six heads:

"Why do you stumble, you old piece of horse flesh? Why do you shake your wings, you heap of feathers? Why does your hair stand on end, you bag of bristles? Think you that Ivan the Bull's Son is here? Why, the lad hasn't been born yet. And even if he has, *he is not fit to do battle with a man of mettle.* I'll put him on the palm of one hand and strike him with my other hand, and nothing will be left of him."

At this, Ivan the Bull's Son leapt out from under the bridge.

"Do not brag, evil one!" he cried. "First catch a falcon and then pluck his feathers. First fight a man of stout heart, aye, and vanquish him, and then revile him. Let us cross swords, and he who overcomes the other will boast of his prowess."

They came together and crossed swords with such force that the ground beneath them quaked and groaned. And it was Chudo-Yudo who got the worst of it, for Ivan the Bull's Son smote off three of his heads with one blow.

"Stay, Ivan the Bull's Son, stay and let me rest!" he begged.

"Rest not, Chudo-Yudo, for you have three heads and I have but one. When only one head is left you, then will we rest," said Ivan the Bull's Son.

They came together and crossed swords again, and Ivan the Bull's Son smote off Chudo-Yudo's other three heads. Then he cut up his body into small pieces, threw them into the Currant River, laid the six heads under the Cranberry Bridge and himself went back to the hut.

Morning came, and there was Prince Ivan at the door.

"Well, did you see anything to alarm you?" Ivan the Bull's Son asked him.

"No, not even a fly flew past me."

On the following night it was Ivan the Cook's Son who went to keep watch, but he too lay down behind some bushes and fell asleep. Now, Ivan the Bull's

Son felt that he could not put much trust in him. He waited till it was past midnight, and then, taking his sword and shield, stepped outside and stationed himself under the Cranberry Bridge.

All of a sudden waves rose on the river, the eagles sitting on the tops of the oak-trees uttered a shrill cry, and Chudo-Yudo the Dragon, he of the nine heads, came riding up. His horse stumbled under him, the black raven perching on his shoulder shook his wings, and the hunting dog that ran behind him bristled, and Chudo-Yudo raised his whip and sent it whistling over the horse's flanks, the raven's wings and the dog's ears.

"Why do you stumble, you old piece of horse flesh? Why do you shake your wings, you heap of feathers? Why does your hair stand on end, you bag of bristles?" he roared. "Think you that Ivan the Bull's Son is here? Well, he hasn't been born yet, and even if he has, *he is not fit to do battle with a man of mettle.* Why, I'll kill him with one finger!"

At this Ivan the Bull's Son leapt out from under the bridge.

"Wait, brag not, evil one!" he cried. "*First wash your hands and pray to the Lord and only then take up your sword.* None knows yet who is to be the victor!"

He waved his sharp sword once and then again and smote off six of Chudo-Yudo's heads. But Chudo-Yudo struck him in return and drove him knee-deep into the ground.

This did not daunt Ivan the Bull's Son. He picked up a handful of sand and flung it into his foe's face, and as Chudo-Yudo was rubbing his eyes, trying to get the sand out of them, the youth smote off the rest of his heads, cut up his body into small pieces, threw them into the river and laid his nine heads under the bridge.

Morning came, and there was Ivan the Cook's Son at the door.

"Well, did you see anything to alarm you?" Ivan the Bull's Son asked.

"No, not a fly flew past me, not a gnat went piping by."

Ivan the Bull's Son led his brothers under the Cranberry Bridge, showed them the dragons' heads and said:

"You loafers you! *It's not for you to do battle or the plains to rove, but to lie on a ledge above the stove.*"

The third night came, and Ivan the Bull's Son prepared to go out to keep watch. He took a towel, hung it on the wall, and placing a bowl on the floor beneath it, said:

"I am off to do battle to the death! And you, my brothers, must stay awake and never take your eyes off the towel. Blood will start running from it, but if it fills half the bowl or even the whole of it, think nothing of it. It is only if the blood flows over the edges that you must untether my horse and yourselves haste to my side."

Ivan the Bull's Son placed himself under the Cranberry Bridge, and just after midnight, waves rose on the river, the eagles sitting on the tops of the oak-trees uttered a shrill cry, and Chudo-Yudo the Dragon, he of the twelve heads, came riding up on a horse that had twelve wings, a coat of silver and a tail and mane of gold. Chudo-Yudo spurred him on, and the horse stumbled, the black raven perching on the dragon's shoulder shook his wings, and the hunting dog that ran behind him bristled.

At this Chudo-Yudo waved his whip and sent it whistling over the horse's flanks, the raven's wings and the dog's ears.

"Why do you stumble, you old piece of horse flesh? Why do you shake your wings, you heap of feathers? Why does your hair stand on end, you bag of bristles?" he roared. "Think you that Ivan the Bull's Son is here? Well, he hasn't been born yet. And even if he has, *he's not fit to do battle with a man of mettle.* All I need do is blow at him, and nothing, not even a handful of dust, will be left of him."

At this Ivan the Bull's Son leapt out from under the bridge and faced Chudo-Yudo.

"Wait, do not boast!" he cried. *"First wash your hands and pray to the Lord, and only then take up your sword."*

"Ah, so it's you, Ivan the Bull's Son! What brings you here?"

"I am here to take a look at you, evil one, and to test your strength."

"To test my strength? You're not up to it, my lad, you are as a flea beside me!"

"I am not here to tell tales or to hear you tell yours," said Ivan the Bull's Son. "I am here to fight you to the death!"

And he waved his sword and smote off three of Chudo-Yudo's heads. But Chudo-Yudo caught them up and passed his fiery finger over them, and all three of them grew fast to the necks again just as if they had never been smitten off at all. And now Ivan the Bull's Son fared badly, for Chudo-Yudo got the better of him and drove him knee-deep into the ground.

"Stay, evil one!" Ivan the Bull's Son cried. "Even when one tsar fights another they sometimes call for a truce and take a rest. Are you and I better than they that we should fight without respite?"

Chudo-Yudo agreed that they should stop fighting and rest a while, and Ivan the Bull's Son pulled off his right glove and sent it flying at the hut where he had left his brothers. The glove hit the windows and smashed them, but the two brothers slept and heard nothing.

Ivan the Bull's Son then waved his sword harder and smote off six of Chudo-Yudo's heads. But Chudo-Yudo caught them up and passed his fiery finger over them, and all the heads grew fast to the necks again. Then he fell on Ivan the Bull's Son and drove him waist-deep into the ground.

Now, Ivan the Bull's Son was wise, and he asked Chudo-Yudo to stop fighting and let him rest a while. To this Chudo-Yudo agreed, and Ivan the Bull's Son pulled off his left glove and sent it flying at the hut. The glove crashed through the roof, but the two brothers slept on and heard nothing, so he waved his sword for the third time and smote off nine of Chudo-Yudo's heads. But Chudo-Yudo caught them up, he passed his fiery finger over them, and they grew fast to the necks again. Then he fell on Ivan the Bull's Son and drove him shoulder-deep into the ground.

But Ivan the Bull's Son asked him to let him rest again, and when Chudo-Yudo agreed to this, he took off his helmet and sent it flying at the hut. The hut fell to pieces, and the logs it was built of *rolled over the ground with a mighty sound.*

Only then did the brothers wake. They looked about them and saw that blood filled the bowl to the brim and flowed over its edges and that their brother's horse, neighing loudly, was straining at the chains he was tethered with. They rushed to the stable and untethered him and themselves made for the bridge.

"So you have tricked me!" Chudo-Yudo roared. "It seems there are those at hand who would help you."

Now Ivan's great steed came galloping up and struck Chudo-Yudo with his hooves, and this gave Ivan the Bull's Son time to climb out of the ground. He was quick and at once cut off Chudo-Yudo's fiery finger and then went at the dragon's heads. He smote off every one of them, cut up the dragon's body into small pieces and threw them all into the Currant River.

Only then was he joined by his two brothers.

"You are loafers, both of you!" said Ivan the Bull's Son. "I nearly paid with my life because you could not stay awake."

Came the dawn, and Ivan the Bull's Son strode out into the open field, flung himself on the ground and turned into a sparrow. And it was in this guise that he flew up to the palace of white stone where the three dragons had lived. He perched on a windowsill, and the old witch, the dragons' mother-in-law, saw him, threw him a handful of grain and said:

"*Peck away, little bird, at this yellow grain while I pour out my sorrow and speak of my pain.* Ivan the Bull's Son has brought misfortune to me and mine, he has slain all my three sons-in-law!"

"Do not grieve, Mother, we will pay him back for everything!" her three daughters, the wives of the dragons said.

"I am going to make Ivan the Bull's Son and his two brothers very, very hungry, and then out I'll come on the road and turn myself into an apple-tree with apples of gold and silver growing on it," said the youngest of the three. "And he who plucks one of them and eats of it will drop dead."

"I am going to make Ivan the Bull's Son and his two brothers very, very thirsty and myself turn into a well with two dippers, one of gold and the other of silver, floating on top of it," said the middle daughter. "And he who touches either of the dippers will drown."

"As for me," said the eldest daughter, "I am going to make Ivan the Bull's Son and his two brothers feel very sleepy and myself turn into a bed of gold. And he who lies down on it will be burnt to death."

Ivan the Bull's Son heard out all they had to say, flew quickly away and turned back into the tall and handsome lad he had been before. And the three brothers mounted their steeds and rode home.

On they rode along the road, and as the hours passed, began to feel faint with hunger. All of a sudden there before them they saw an apple-tree, its branches heavy with gold and silver apples. Prince Ivan and Ivan the Cook's Son urged on their steeds in the hope of plucking an apple, but Ivan the Bull's Son got to the tree ahead of them and began cutting it down, making the blood

58

spurt out of it with every thrust of his sword.

And he did the same with the golden well and the golden bed, killing in this way all three of the witch's daughters.

As soon as the witch learnt of her daughters' death she dressed herself like a beggarwoman, hung a sack on her back, ran out on to the road and stood there. By and by Ivan the Bull's Son and his brothers came riding toward her, and she stretched out her hand and began begging for alms.

"Our father has enough gold and to spare, brother!" said Prince Ivan. "So why don't you give this old beggarwoman a coin or two?"

Ivan the Bull's Son brought out some coins and held them out to the old woman, but instead of taking them she seized him by the hand and vanished together with him. Prince Ivan and Ivan the Cook's Son looked about them, but not seeing either the old woman or their brother, were frightened half out of their wits, and, putting their horses into a gallop, rode home.

And the witch dragged Ivan the Bull's Son to a deep cellar and led him to her husband's bedside.

"Here is the one who slew all who were dear to us!" she said.

Now, the witch's husband, who was lying on a bed of iron, was very, very old, and so long were his lashes and so thick his brows that they hung over his eyes so that he could see nothing. He had twelve mighty knights summoned and said to them:

"Take a pitchfork, my lads, and lift up my brows and lashes so that I can take a look at the one who slew my sons-in-law and see what he is like."

The knights did as he bade, and the old man looked Ivan the Bull's Son over and said:

"Good for you, Ivan, my lad! So it was you that got up the courage to fight my sons-in-law and then slew them! Now speak and tell me what I am to do with you."

"Do with me whatever you like, it's for you to decide," said Ivan the Bull's Son.

"Let us not waste words then, for I cannot bring my children back to life again. Better do me a service. Go to the tsardom-that-never-was-heard-of, to the realm-that-never-was-seen, carry off Queen-Locks of Gold and bring her to me. I wish to marry her."

"You're much too old for that, you old devil, it's young lads like me that ought to marry," Ivan the Bull's Son thought.

And as for the old witch, she was filled with such fury that her wits forsook her, and she tied a stone round her neck, jumped into a river and drowned herself.

"Here is a club for you, Ivan, my lad," the old man said. "Go to such-and-such an oak-tree, strike it thrice with the club and say: 'Open, tree! Out with you, ship!' Repeat these words three times, and as soon as the ship is before you, tell the oak-tree to close, and repeat this three times, too. And mind that you do it all or you'll forfeit my good will."

Ivan the Bull's Son found the oak-tree, struck it with the club over and over again and called out:

"Open, tree! Out with all that is within you!"

At this a ship appeared from out of the tree, and Ivan the Bull's Son got into it, and, calling "Follow me, all!", sailed off down the river.

By and by he glanced back, and there sailing after him, were boats of all kinds, so many that there was no counting them! And all who were in the boats were singing his praises.

By and by an old man rowed up to him.

"Long may you live and long may you prosper, Ivan the Bull's Son!" he said. "You are a man like no other! Take me on board, and I will be a good friend to you."

"What can you do?"

"I can eat, and eat heartily, my lad!"

"The devil take you! That's something I can do, too. But you can join me all the same, for I'm always glad of a friend."

Some time passed, and another old man rowed up to the ship.

"Greetings, Ivan the Bull's Son!" he called. "Do take me on board!"

"What can *you* do?"

"I can drink much ale and much wine, my lad."

"Is that all? But, oh, well, get on board, I'll be glad to have you."

By and by a third old man rowed up to the ship.

"Greetings to you, Ivan the Bull's Son!" he called. "Won't you take me on board too?"

"Tell me what you can do."

"I can steam myself in a bathhouse."

"What the devil! A wise lot, all of you!"

But he took the third old man on board too.

By and by a fourth old man rowed up to the ship.

"Long may you live and long may you prosper, Ivan the Bull's Son!" he called. "Pray take me on board, too."

"And who may you be?"

"An astrologer, my lad."

"An astrologer? Well, there you go me one better, for to count the stars is something I cannot do. So get on board and welcome!"

The fourth old man had only just joined Ivan the Bull's Son when a fifth old man rowed up and asked to be taken on board.

"A plague on the lot of you! What am I to do with you all! Be quick now and tell me what you can do," said Ivan the Bull's Son.

"I can swim like a fish, my lad."

"Well, then, get on board and welcome!"

Off they sailed together to fetch Queen-Locks of Gold, and when they came to the tsardom-never-before-heard-of, the realm-never-before-seen they learnt that Ivan the Bull's Son had long been expected there and for three whole months bread had been baked, wine made and ale brewed in preparation for his coming.

Seeing the wagonloads of bread and of casks of wine and of ale set before him, Ivan the Bull's Son was quite taken aback.

"What does this mean?" he asked.

"All of this is yours to eat and to drink," they told him.

"What the devil! Why, I couldn't eat or drink that much in a year!"

But the next moment he remembered the old men he had with him and called out:

"Come, old men, you who are stout of heart and strong of frame, which of you is a great eater and which a great drinker?"

And Big Eater and Big Drinker called back:

"We are, Ivan the Bull's Son! All that food and drink is as nothing to us!"

"Well, then, set to and prove it!"

At this Big Eater came running up, and it wasn't merely whole loaves but whole wagonloads of bread that he stuffed into his mouth and swallowed. Soon all of the bread was gone, and he shouted:

"Bring more! I'm still hungry!"

Big Drinker was the next to come running up. He began swilling the wine and the ale, and when none was left, swallowed the casks as well.

"Bring more! I'm thirsty still!" he cried.

Now, the servants of Queen-Locks of Gold were quite flustered by this. They ran to see her and they told her that all of the bread and wine was gone. But Queen-Locks of Gold was not at all put out and ordered them to take Ivan the Bull's Son to the bathhouse for him to be steamed there.

Now, the bathhouse had been heated for three months on end, and was now so hot that none could come within a distance of even five miles to it without getting badly burnt. The queen's servants told Ivan the Bull's Son to come with them and be steamed there, but when he saw how hot the bathhouse was he said:

"You must be mad. Why, I'll be burnt to death there!"

But no sooner were the words out of his mouth than he remembered the old men he had with him and called out:

"Come, old men, you who are stout of heart and strong of frame, which of you likes to be steamed in a bathhouse?"

At this the third old man came running up to him.

"I do, my lad!" he cried. "It's as nothing to me."

He ran into the bathhouse, blew into one of its corners and spat into the other, and the bathhouse cooled at once, and snow piled up on the floor.

"I'm freezing!" he shouted. "Heat this bathhouse and don't stop heating it for another three years!"

The servants of Queen-Locks of Gold rushed to her chamber to tell her about it, but Ivan the Bull's Son did not wait for them to come back and demanded that the queen be given up to him.

At this the queen stepped out of her chamber, put her snow-white hand in his and got aboard the ship together with him.

They set sail at once, but when a day and another had passed, Queen-Locks of Gold felt very sad and woebegone. She struck herself on the chest, turned into a star and soared up to the sky.

"I don't suppose I'll ever see her again," said Ivan the Bull's Son. But the next moment he remembered the old men he had with him and called out:

"Come, old men, you who are stout of heart and strong of frame, which of you can count the stars?"

"I can, my lad, it's as nothing to me!" the fourth old man told him.

He flung himself down on the deck, turned into a star, flew up into the sky and began counting the stars. He found one that had not been there before and gave it a push, and it rolled from its place and down the sky, fell on the deck and turned into Queen-Locks of Gold again.

They sailed on, but when a day and another had passed, Queen-Locks of Gold was overcome with sadness. She struck herself on the chest, turned into a pike and swam away.

"Well, I don't suppose I'll ever see her again!" Ivan the Bull's Son told himself, but he remembered the last of the old men and called him to his side.

"Is it not you who can swim like a fish?" he asked.

"Yes, indeed, my lad, it's as nothing to me!" the old man said.

He flung himself on the deck, turned into a fish, slipped into the sea, and going after the pike, pricked it with his spiky fins.

The pike could not bear the pain. It leapt up on to the deck and turned back again into Queen-Locks of Gold.

After this *the five old men, with many a sigh, bade Ivan the Bull's Son a fond goodbye* and went home, and Ivan and Queen-Locks of Gold sailed back to the realm of the father of the three Chudo-Yudos. The old man had twelve mighty knights summoned, and he bade them fetch an iron pitchfork and lift up his brows and lashes.

This they did, and he looked at Queen-Locks of Gold, and, turning to Ivan the Bull's Son, said:

"Well done, Ivan the Bull's Son! *I forgive you and set you free, and you need not fear any vengeance from me.*"

"Stay!" said Ivan the Bull's Son. "Think before you speak."

"What is it now?"

"Well, it's this way. I have had a deep pit dug and a plank laid across it, and *whichever of us crosses the pit, and 'twill take some courage and also some wit,* shall wed Queen-Locks of Gold."

"Very well," the old man said. "Come, Ivan the Bull's Son, you cross the pit first."

Ivan the Bull's Son stepped on to the plank, and Queen-Locks of Gold said half under her breath:

"*Light as a swan's down shall you be and so walk across and marry me!*"

And Ivan the Bull's Son walked across very easily, and the plank did not so much as bend under him. But when the old man tried to do the same, he stumbled when he was halfway across and fell into the pit.

After this Ivan the Bull's Son went home, taking Queen-Locks of Gold with him. They were married soon after, *and so rich a feast was the one they held as never before had been beheld!* There sat Ivan the Bull's Son at the table, and he said to his brothers:

"*Long did I fight and far did I sail, and by my bride's side all other maids pale*! As for you, my brothers, loafers that you are, *you'd better sit on that stove ledge yonder and chew at bricks to everyone's wonder*!"

* * *

Now, I was at that feast too. *I drank strong ale and stronger wine, and all of it ran down this beard of mine,* and none got into my mouth! And oh, the many good things they treated me to! *They took his pail of slops from a bull and gave it to me with milk filled full. I drained it all and ate a bun that was soaked in the milk and dried in the sun. I could not refuse however I tried, for they knocked me down with a punch in my side. A cap with bells I then put on, and they pushed me out and cried,* "Begone!"

Translated by Irina Zheleznova

Princess
Never-A-Smile

How big is this world of ours! There is room enough in it for the rich and the poor, and the Lord cares for and judges us all. Some live in comfort, some know nothing save misfortune and toil—to each his lot!

Now, Princess Never-A-Smile lived in princely chambers, in a lofty palace in ease and luxury and could have whatever her heart desired, but she never smiled and never laughed, and it was as if nothing gave her joy.

It grieved her father the king to see her so sad, so he opened wide the doors of his palace to young men of all stations. "Try to make the princess laugh," said he. "Anyone who succeeds shall have her in marriage." At once great numbers of those who were tempted to try and win the princess began gathering by the palace. From early morn till late at night they all came pouring through the gate. Among them were kings and princes, boyars and nobles, soldiers and commoners. *Feasts were held, mead was drunk and ale, and still the princess stayed wan and pale.* And she never once smiled.

Now, in a distant part of the realm there lived a good and honest man, a simple workingman. He kept the yard clean and tended the cattle and was at work from morn till night. And his master, who was a rich man but a just one, always paid him promptly. One day, the man's year of service being up, the master put a bag of money on the table, and saying "Help yourself, take as

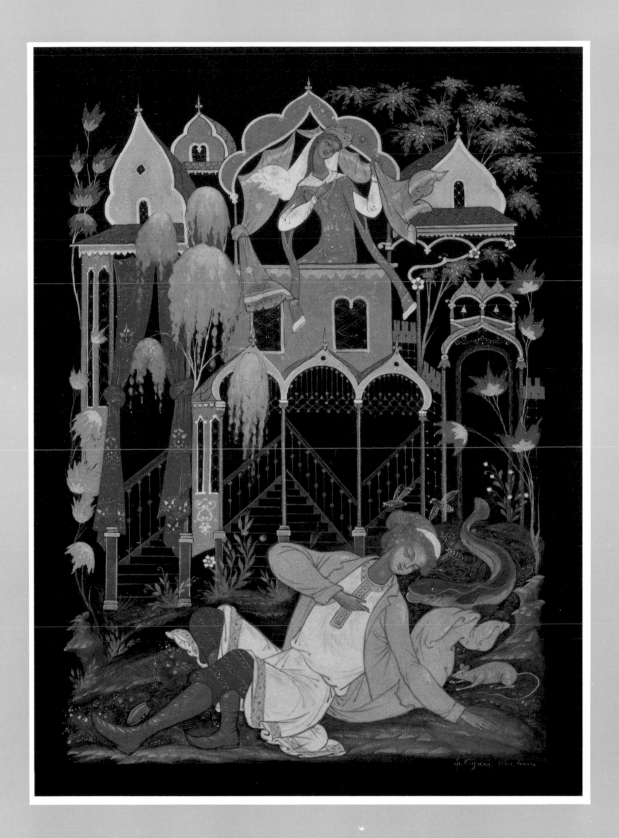

much as you want!" left the room. The man went up to the table and stood there, lost in thought, not wanting to take more than he had earned. In the end he took a single coin, but a little while later, as he was bending over a well in order to scoop up a handful of water and have a sip, the coin slipped out of his hand and sank to the well bottom.

The man was left penniless. Another would have wept or, in his bitterness, put all thought of work aside, but not he. "It's all God's will," said he to himself. "He knows whom to make rich and from whom to take his last penny. It must be that I did not do my best, I'll work harder from now on!" And he set to work and did whatever he set out to do quickly and well.

Another year went by. The man's second term of service was up, and his master put a bag of money on the table, and saying "Help yourself, take as much as you want!" left the room. The man again stood there thinking, unwilling to take more than he had earned. In the end he took one coin, but a little while later, as he was bending over a well in order to scoop up a handful of water and have a sip, the coin slipped out of his hand and sank to the well bottom. This only made him work the harder, so hard, in fact, that in his zeal he often went without sleep and forgot to eat. Some *let their wheat whither in the field, but not so he who tripled the yield*; other men's cows might sicken but not so those he tended *who had hides like silk and gave plenty of milk*; other men's horses might have to be dragged uphill, but not those he cared for *who were given their head and forged ahead.*

The months passed, and now the man's third year of service was up, and his master, who knew to whom he owed his well-being, put a bag of money on the table. "Help yourself!" he said. "You worked hard and deserve to be paid well." And with these words he left the room. The man only took one coin again as he had before, but when he came up to the well for a drink of water he saw that the two coins he had lost were floating on top. He knew that this was God's way of rewarding him for his labours and felt very happy. "It's time for me to take a look at the world and see how other people live," said he to himself. And away he went where the road led. He was walking across a field when he saw a mouse running toward him. "My good man, my dear friend, give me a silver coin and don't grudge it, for I may be of help to you too some day!" said the mouse. The man gave it a silver coin and went on, and as he was walking across a forest he saw a beetle crawling toward him. "My good man, my dear friend, give me a silver coin and don't grudge it, for I may be of help to you too some day!" said the beetle. The man gave it a silver coin and went on, and as he was wading across a stream he saw a sheatfish swimming toward him. "My good man, my dear friend, give me a silver coin and don't grudge it, for I may be of help to you too some day!" said the sheatfish. And he did not stop to think but gave it his last coin.

By and by he came to a great city, *and oh, the roofs, and oh, the steeples, and oh, the multitudes of people!* The man did not know where to look. Now, before him there rose the king's own palace, and at the window sat Princess Never-A-Smile and stared straight at him. *He felt quite dizzy and all in a muddle, and down he fell straight into a puddle!* And lo and behold!—as if out of thin air the sheatfish, the mouse and the beetle appeared. *They hurried to him and helped him up and bustled about with never a stop. Crunch-Munch the Mouse brushed off his coat, the beetle his shoes, as I'd have you note, and the sheatfish who was of a giant size with its great big whiskers waved off the flies.* Princess Never-A-Smile sat there watching them for a time, and so funny did they look that she burst out laughing. "Who has made my daughter laugh?" the king asked. "I did!" someone in the crowd shouted. "No, I did!" cried another. "It was neither of them," said Princess Never-A-Smile. "It was that man there!" She pointed at the workingman, and he was at once led into the palace and stood there facing the king and looking as brave and bold as the best of them! The king kept his word, as I have heard, and let him wed his daughter Princess Never-A-Smile. And please don't think our hero dreamt it all. *Believe me you, the story is true!*

Translated by Irina Zheleznova

The Rooster
and the Millstones

Once upon a time there lived an old man and an old woman who were as poor as poor can be. One day they went to the forest, gathered a bagful of acorns, brought them home and set to eating them. Whether it took them long or not to eat them all nobody knows, but the old woman happened to drop an acorn, and it rolled into the cellar and gave off a shoot that grew and grew till it reached the cellar top.

The old woman saw it and said: "Look here, old man, we had better cut through the floor to let the oak grow. We'll soon have it here, and then we won't need to go to the forest for acorns, we'll pick them in the house." The old man cut a hole in the floor, and the shoot, which had turned into a tree by then, grew and grew till it reached the ceiling. The old man took off a part of the ceiling and then of the roof, and the oak went on growing and did not stop till it had reached the sky. By that time the old man and the old woman had eaten all of the acorns in the house, so the old man took a sack and started climbing the oak.

He climbed and he climbed, and lo!—found himself in the sky. He walked over it for a long time and there, sitting before him, he saw a rooster. *He was glossy of head and his comb was red,* and near him lay a pair of millstones. The old man did not stop to think, but, taking both the rooster and the millstones, climbed down the tree. "What are you and I going to eat, old woman?" he asked. "Now wait, just let me see if these millstones turn well or not," said the

old woman. She began turning the millstones round and round, and at every turn out came a pie and a pancake. She went on doing it, and soon there were enough pies and pancakes for a hearty meal. Now both she and the old man could eat their fill whenever they wanted to.

One day a noble came driving past their house, and he stopped and asked if they could give him something to eat. "I can only offer you some pies and pancakes," said the old woman. She started turning the millstones, and out dropped some pies and pancakes. The noble ate them all and then asked the old woman to sell him the millstones, but when she said that she could not do it, he stole them from her. Seeing that the millstones were gone, the old man and the old woman began wailing and weeping. "Don't you wail or weep!" said Glossy Head-Comb So Red. "I'll get the millstones back!" And away he flew straight for the noble's house. He perched on top of the gate and sang out: "Cock-a-doodle-doo! Come, noble, give us back our millstones! *They are blue and gold, as you need not be told.*" The noble heard the rooster and bade his servants drown him. The servants caught Glossy Head-Comb So Red and threw him down a well, but Glossy Head-Comb So Red sang out: "Come, beak, drink up the water! Come, beak, drink up the water!" And he put down his beak and drank and drank till the well was quite dry. After that he flew to the noble's house, and, perching on the balcony, sang out again: "Cock-a-doodle-doo! Come, noble, give us back our millstones! *They are blue and gold, as you need not be told.*" Hearing him, the noble bade his cook catch him and bake him in a hot oven. The cook caught Glossy Head-Comb So Red and threw him straight into the fire, but Glossy Head-Comb So Red sang out: "Come, beak, douse the flames! Come, beak, douse the flames!" and the water came pouring out of his beak. The fire was soon put out, and Glossy Head-Comb So Red flew into the noble's house and sang out again: "Cock-a-doodle-doo! Come, noble, give us back our millstones! *They are blue and gold, as you need not be told.*" The noble's guests were frightened and rushed out of the house, the noble went running after them to try and get them to come back, and Glossy Head-Comb So Red seized the millstones and flew with them to the house of the old man and old woman.

Translated by Irina Zheleznova

The Tsar Maiden

In a certain kingdom, in a certain realm there lived a merchant. His wife died, and he had no one left in the world save his son Ivan. Some time passed, and the merchant married again and hired a servant to take care of Ivan. Now, Ivan had grown to manhood by then and was a most handsome youth, and his stepmother fell in love with him. One day, accompanied by his servant, Ivan set out on a raft to catch fish at sea. All of a sudden they saw, sailing toward them, thirty ships, with the Tsar Maiden and thirty other maids, her chosen sisters, on board. As soon as the raft drew close to the ships, all thirty of them cast anchor, and Ivan and his servant were invited to join the Tsar Maiden. She and her thirty chosen sisters greeted them joyfully, and the Tsar Maiden told Ivan that she had seen him once before, had fallen in love with him and had now come specially to see him. They plighted their troth then and there, and the Tsar Maiden told Ivan to meet her at sea, at the selfsame time, in the selfsame spot, on the following day. She bade him goodbye and sailed away, and Ivan came back home, had his supper and went to bed. While he slept, his stepmother got his servant to come to her chamber, plied him with wine and asked him if Ivan and he had met with any adventures while at sea. The servant told her all about everything, and she gave him a pin and told him to stick it in Ivan's coat as soon as the ships were sighted.

On the following morning, no sooner was Ivan up than he put off to sea on his raft, and his servant did as the stepmother bade, and, seeing the ships come

71

sailing up, stuck the pin in Ivan's coat. This made Ivan feel very, very sleepy, and he said to his servant: "I think I'll lie down and have a nap. Be sure to wake me when the ships sail up nearer." "I shall certainly do that," said the servant. The ships drew close and came to anchor, and the Tsar Maiden sent for Ivan, bidding him join her without delay. But so sound was his sleep that though they nudged him and called his name they could not wake him.

The Tsar Maiden bade Ivan's servant tell Ivan to be in the selfsame spot on the next day, and then she ordered the crew to weigh anchor and hoist the sails. The thirty ships had no sooner set sail than the servant pulled out the pin he had stuck into Ivan's coat, and Ivan at once woke, sprang to his feet and began shouting to the Tsar Maiden to turn back. But as she was far away by then and did not hear him, he came back home and was very sad and crestfallen. As for the stepmother, she again got his servant to come to her chamber, plied him with drink, queried him about all that had taken place that day and bade him stick the pin in Ivan's coat again on the following day. This he did, and Ivan again slept so soundly while at sea that he never saw the Tsar Maiden, who asked that he be told to make a last attempt to meet her in the selfsame spot on the next day.

The third day came, and Ivan and his servant put off to sea again. They sailed up to the selfsame spot, and as soon as he saw the ships sailing toward them, the servant stuck the pin in Ivan's coat. The Tsar Maiden sent for her betrothed, but he was sound asleep and though they did everything they could to wake him, they did not succeed and he never saw her. But she learnt of his stepmother's wiles and his servant's treachery and wrote Ivan a letter, telling him to chop off the servant's head and if he loved her, to seek her beyond the thrice-nine lands in the thrice-ten kingdom.

No sooner had the ships set sail than Ivan's servant pulled the pin out of his coat, and Ivan woke and began calling to the Tsar Maiden to come back. But she was far away by then and though he called at the top of his voice, she did not hear him. The servant gave him her letter, and Ivan read it, and, seizing his sharp sabre, cut off the villain's head. Then he made for shore, bade his father goodbye and set out to seek the thrice-ten kingdom.

He went where the road led, and whether a short or a long time passed nobody knows, for a tale is short in the telling while a deed is long in the doing, but he came at last to a wide field where, turning round and round, stood a hut on chicken feet. He stepped inside, and there before him was Baba-Yaga the Leg of Stone. "Fee-fo-fum!" said she. "Russian blood, Russian flesh! Never did I smell it, never did I see it before. Have you come here of your own free will or at another's bidding, my brave lad?" "At another's bidding, but that was the way I wanted it," Ivan said. "Do you know how I am to get to the thrice-ten kingdom, Grandma?" "No, I don't," Baba-Yaga said, "but my sister might." And she told him to go and see her middle sister.

Ivan thanked her and went on. He walked and he walked, and whether a short or a long time passed nobody knows, but by and by he came to another hut that looked just like the first one. He stepped inside, and there before him was another witch, Baba-Yaga's middle sister. "Fee-fo-fum!" said she. "Russian

73

blood, Russian flesh! Never did I smell it, never did I see it before. Have you come here of your own free will or at another's bidding, my brave lad?" "At another's bidding, but that was the way I wanted it," Ivan said. "Do you know how I am to get to the thrice-ten kingdom, Grandma?" "No, I don't, but go to see my younger sister, for she may know," Baba-Yaga said. "And just remember this: if you anger her and she makes to eat you up, ask her for her three trumpets. She will give them to you, and you must blow the first one softly, the second one louder, and the third one very loudly indeed." And Ivan thanked Baba-Yaga and went on.

He walked and he walked, and whether a short or a long time passed nobody knows, but there before him in the open field, turning round and round, stood a hut on chicken feet. He stepped inside and was met by the third of the Baba-Yagas. "Fee-fo-fum! Russian blood, Russian flesh! Never did I smell it, never did I see it before!" said Baba-Yaga, and off she ran to sharpen her teeth, for she wanted to eat up Ivan. But Ivan got her to give him her three trumpets, and he blew the first one softly, the second one louder, and the third one very loudly indeed, and lo and behold!—birds of all kinds came flying toward him from all sides. The Fire-Bird was among them, and it told him to get on its back. "Make haste or Baba-Yaga will eat you up!" it said. "I'll take you wherever you wish to go." Ivan got on its back, and he was just in time, for there was Baba-Yaga running after them. She caught the Fire-Bird by the tail and pulled out many of its feathers, but the Fire-Bird broke free and went flying away with Ivan on its back. It flew across the skies for a long time, and it came to the ocean-sea. "The thrice-ten kingdom lies beyond the ocean-sea, Ivan," it said. "I haven't the strength to carry you across, so you must try to find a way of getting there by yourself." And Ivan climbed down off the Fire-Bird's back, thanked it and went on along the shore.

He walked and he walked, and, coming to a hut, stepped inside. A very old woman met him, she gave him food and drink and asked him where he was going, and he told her that he was on his way to the thrice-ten kingdom where he hoped to find his betrothed, the Tsar Maiden. "Ah, but the Tsar Maiden does not love you any more, she will kill you if she sees you," said the old woman. "Her love is hid far away." "How am I to find it, Grandma?" "Be patient and wait a while. My daughter, who promised to come to see me today, is a servant of hers, and you may be able to learn what you want to know from her." And the old woman turned Ivan into a pin and stuck the pin in the wall. It was evening when her daughter came flying to see her, and the old woman asked her if she knew where the Tsar Maiden's love was hid. "No, I don't," said the daughter, "but I will try to get the Tsar Maiden herself to tell me where." She flew away, but was back on the following day. "I have learnt where the Tsar Maiden's love is hid," said she. "There is an oak growing on the opposite shore of the ocean-sea, and in the oak there is a chest, in the chest a hare, in the hare a duck, in the duck an egg, and in the egg the Tsar-Maiden's love."

Ivan heard her out, and then he took some bread and set out for the opposite shore of the ocean-sea. He found the oak-tree, took down the chest, got the hare out of the chest, the duck out of the hare, and the egg out of the duck, and went back to the old woman's hut. Now, soon after that it was the old woman's name-day, and she invited the Tsar Maiden and the thirty maids, her chosen sisters, to be her guests. She baked the egg Ivan had brought, and Ivan she dressed in festive garb and hid in her chamber.

Noon arrived, and the Tsar Maiden and her thirty chosen sisters came flying to the old woman's hut. The old woman seated them at the table and laid out a royal feast for them, and when they had eaten and drunk she gave each of them an egg, to the thirty maids ordinary ones, and to the Tsar Maiden the one Ivan had brought. The Tsar Maiden ate her egg, and she fell madly in love with Ivan. The old woman led him out from his hiding-place, and oh, how happy he and the Tsar Maiden were! Away they went together to the Tsar-Maiden's kingdom and were married soon after. *They knew no woe, shed never a tear and prospered the more from year to year.*

Translated by Irina Zheleznova

The Lad Who Knew
the Language
of Birds

In a certain town there once lived a merchant and his wife who had a son named Vassily, a lad wise beyond his years. One day the three of them were having dinner together when the nightingale they kept in a cage hanging over the table burst into song. So sorrowfully did it sing that the merchant found it hard to bear and said: "If there were someone who could tell me what the nightingale's song is about, I would give him half my property and make him heir to most of my belongings."

Now, Vassily, who was then only six years old, looked at his mother and father, and looked again. "I know what the nightingale's song is about," he said, "but I'm afraid to tell you."

"Speak up and don't keep anything from us!" the mother and father cried, and Vassily, whose eyes had filled with tears, said: "The nightingale says that one day you two will come to serve me: you, Father, will bring water for me to wash, and you, Mother, a towel for me to wipe myself."

These words cut the mother and father to the quick, and they decided to get rid of their son. They built a small boat, and one night, when it was quite dark, put the sleeping lad in it, and set it afloat. But they never saw the nightingale fly out of its cage and after the boat and perch on the lad's shoulder.

The boat drifted farther and farther away, and when it was far out at sea it was sighted by the captain of a ship coming in full sail toward it. The captain

took pity on Vassily, and learning of his plight, said that he would care for him as for his own son.

On the following day the nightingale began singing, and the lad said to the captain: "The nightingale is warning us. It says that a storm is brewing that will smash the masts and tear the sails and that we had better seek cover."

The captain shrugged his shoulders in disbelief, but before long a storm did indeed break, and it smashed the masts and tore the sails. But what was past was past, so they set up new masts, and, having patched the sails, got under way. Some time passed, and Vassily, who had been listening to the nightingale, said that it had told him that twelve pirate ships were sailing toward them and that if they did not take care they were in danger of being captured. This time the captain heeded the warning. He hid the ship in the lee of an island and watched the pirate ships glide past, and it was only when they were out of sight that he put to sea again.

Whether a short or a long time passed nobody knows, but the ship docked in the port city of Khvalinsk, and it came to the ears of the captain and his crew that for several years now three ravens had been circling in front of the royal palace, their loud cawing giving the king no peace. The palace windows were kept tightly shut, and everything, even to firing a gun at them, had been tried to drive the birds away, but nothing helped. The king had at last had a notice put up on every city street and every wharf which said that he who found a way of driving off the ravens could have the princess in marriage and half the kingdom besides. But as for those who undertook to do it and did not succeed, they would have their heads cut off. Now, though there had been many willing to marry the princess, not one had been able to drive off the ravens, and they had all died on the block.

Vassily now began begging the captain to let him go to the king and try to drive away the ravens. The captain was horrified, but as the lad would not listen to him, he told him that he could do as he liked, and would have only himself to blame if he fared badly.

Vassily came to the palace, spoke to the king and asked him to have the windows of the palace thrown open. This was done, and he stood there listening to the ravens cawing and then said: "You can see for yourself, Your Majesty, that there are just three ravens there, a he-raven, a she-raven and a fledgling. Now, the mother and father birds are arguing about which of them is to have the fledgling, and they want you, Your Majesty, to decide between them."

The king thought this over.

"Let the father bird have the fledgling," said he, and no sooner had he uttered these words than the three birds all flew away, the father bird and the fledgling in one direction, and the mother bird, in the opposite one.

After that the king took Vassily under his wing, had him live in the palace and showered many favours upon him. The years passed, and the lad, who grew up to be a tall and handsome youth, married the princess and got half the kingdom for his own. But some time passed, and he decided to go to distant lands to see how the people there lived. He set off on his travels, and it was when he had been on his way for some months that he stopped for the night in a strange city. Morning came, and when he asked for some water, it was the master of the house who brought it and poured it for him, and his wife who handed Vassily a towel. They set to talking, and Vassily soon discovered that the two were none other but his own mother and father. He fell at their feet with tears of joy, and, cutting short his journey, took them back to Khvalinsk with him. *And there they all lived in good health and good cheer and prospered the more with each passing year.*

Translated by Irina Zheleznova

The Enchanted
Princess

In a certain kingdom there was once a soldier who served with the royal horse guards for twenty-five years. And the king rewarded him for his honesty and faithful service by allowing him to retire and giving him the horse he had had while with the regiment together with its saddle and harness. The soldier bade his comrades goodbye and set out for home. He rode for a week and another and a third and was still on the way when he found that he had run out of all his money and had not enough left to buy food for either himself or his horse. The journey ahead of him was long, and, being very hungry, he began looking round him for a place to spend the night. He looked and he looked, and he saw a large castle looming just ahead. "I had better go to that castle and ask to be given work to do, I may be able to earn something that way," said he to himself.

He turned down the road leading to the castle, rode into the courtyard, led his horse into the stable, and, having given it some fodder, made for the castle door. He stepped inside, and there before him was a table on which stood jugs of wine and platters of food of a kind to please any palate! The soldier ate and drank his fill, and he had just told himself that it was time to have a good sleep when a she-bear lumbered into the room. "Have no fear of me, soldier!" said she. "No one here will harm you. I am not a bear but a princess in a bear's guise. If you are stout of heart enough and agree to spend three nights in the castle, then the spell cast over me will break, and I will get back my human shape and marry you."

The soldier agreed to do as she asked, and the bear went away, leaving him alone. No sooner was she gone, however, than he began to feel very, very sad and troubled, and as time passed the feeling grew so strong that if not for the wine to which he kept helping himself he would have fled before the first night was up. The second day came and then the third, and the soldier told himself that he could bear it no longer and tried to run away, but wherever he went he found himself up against thick walls and could not find a way out of the castle. There was nothing to be done, and he was forced to remain there for the third night, but when morning came a most beautiful princess appeared before him, thanked him for having stayed there as she had asked and said that she was ready to marry him if he wished. They were married then and there and began living together very happily—*there was nothing to grieve them or make them feel sad, and a right merry time the two of them had.*

The months passed, and the soldier remembered his homeland and was filled with an urge to see it again. And though the princess begged him not to go and leave her, saying that he had everything his heart desired right there, he would not listen to her. They took leave of one another, and she gave him a little bag filled with seeds and said: "No matter where you go, you must throw these seeds to either side of the road. For wherever a seed falls, a tree will at once spring up, its branches heavy with fruit, and there will be song-birds perching in it and singing their songs and a cat walking round it and telling tales of far-away lands." The soldier mounted his old, trusty steed and set out on his way, and no matter where he went he would throw handfuls of seeds to either side of the road, and whole forests rose in his wake, the trees seeming to shoot up out of the ground.

On he rode for a day and another and a third, and a field spread before him. A caravan stood there and a group of merchants sat on the grass in a circle playing cards. A pot with something cooking in it hung from a pole beside them. "A miracle if ever there was one!" said the soldier to himself. "The pot is sending off clouds of steam, but there is no fire under it. I had better come closer and get a better look at it." And he turned off the road and rode up to the merchants. "Good day to you, honest folk!" said he, and it never entered his head that the merchants were not merchants at all but evil spirits. "That's a fine pot you have there, but I have something that is better still." He took a seed out of his bag and cast it on the ground, and the same moment a tree grew up out of it. Its branches were heavy with fruit, there were song-birds perching on them and singing away, and round it there walked a cat and told tales of far-away lands. This was enough for the evil spirits who knew at once who the man before them was. "Why, it was he who freed the princess," said they. "Let us give him our magic potion to drink, for then he will fall asleep and not wake for six months." They offered the soldier their potion, he drank it and fell into a deep sleep, and the evil spirits vanished together with their caravan and their pot.

Soon after this the princess went for a walk in her garden, and she saw that the tops of the trees there had withered. "That is a bad sign!" said she. "Some-

81

thing must have happened to my husband. Three months have now passed, and he is not back yet." And off she set from home to seek him. She rode along the road he had followed, and there were forests towering on either side of it, with song-birds singing away in the trees and cats walking round them purring and telling tales of far-away lands. Soon, however, the forests were left behind her, and the road wound across a wide field. "Where could my husband be?" the princess asked herself. "It's as though the earth had swallowed him." She glanced about her, and her eye fell on a tree that looked just like the trees in the forest. And there, lying beneath it, was her own dear husband.

The princess ran up to him and began trying to wake him. She nudged and pinched him and even pricked him with a pin, but he felt no pain and lay there like one dead. The princess was vexed. "May the wild winds seize you and carry you off none knows where!" cried she. And no sooner had she uttered these terrible words than the winds began whistling and blowing, and they caught up the soldier and carried him off and away. The princess burst into tears. But though she cursed herself for having said what she had she could not bring her husband back. So home she went and began living there all by herself.

As for the soldier, he had been carried far, far away, beyond the thrice-nine lands, to the thrice-ten kingdom, and thrown on to a spit of land that stretched between two seas. He fell on its very tip, which was very narrow, so that if he so much as stirred he was in danger of falling in the water. Luckily for him, however, he slept without moving a finger and so remained unharmed. Six months passed, and the soldier woke and looked about him. On either side of him the waves rose, and the sea stretched away without end. "By what miracle did I get here, who could have brought me here?" he asked himself. He turned and walked along the spit and soon found himself on an island with a tall, steep mountain rising on it, its tip touching the clouds. On top of the mountain lay a large stone.

He came up to the mountain and saw three devils fighting each other at its foot, the blood streaming from the many gashes on their bodies and tufts of hair flying about them. "Stop, you fiends! Why are you fighting?" the soldier cried. "Well, it's like this," the devils said. "Our father died two days ago, he left us three magic things, the flying carpet, the seven-league boots, and the invisible cap, and we cannot agree as to which of us is to get which." "A curse on you, to be starting a fight because of such nonsense! I can divide the things among you if you like, and I won't hurt anyone's feelings." "Go ahead, then, do it, friend!" "Very well. Be quick now and go to the pine forests, get a hundred poods of resin each and bring it here." The devils hurried to obey him. They rushed to the pine forests, got the resin and brought it to him. "Now fetch me the biggest pot you have in hell," the soldier said. Away ran the devils again and were back soon, dragging a huge pot. This they filled to the top with resin, forty whole barrels of it. And the soldier made up a fire and as soon as the resin melted, ordered the devils to drag the pot up the mountain and pour it over it. The devils did as he bade. "Do you see that stone there, on top of the mountain?" the

soldier asked. "Push it and let it roll downhill, and then the three of you run after it. He who is the first to overtake and seize hold of it can choose whichever of the three magic things he wants; he who comes after him can take either one of the two left; and he who comes last will have to be satisfied with the last one." The devils hastened to do as he said. They gave the stone a push, and as it went rolling down the mountain, they rushed after it. One of them seized it, but the stone overturned, and the devil fell on his back and was caught under it. The same thing happened to the second and the third devil, and they all three stuck fast to the resin and could not move! Seeing them lying there, the soldier slipped the seven-league boots and the invisible cap under his arm, and, getting on the flying carpet, flew off to seek his kingdom.

Whether a short or a long time passed nobody knows, but by and by he came flying up to a hut. He stepped inside, and whom should he see sitting there but *Baba-Yaga the Leg of Stone, a very, very old and toothless crone.* "Greetings to you, Grandma!" the soldier said. "Can you tell me how I am to find my beautiful princess?" "No, my man, that I can't. Never did I see her, never did I hear of her. Go beyond so many seas and so many lands, for that is where my sister lives, and ask her about it. She knows more about everything than I do and may be able to help you."

The soldier got on his flying carpet, away he flew, and he travelled over the world for a long, long time. And whenever he was hungry or thirsty he would put on the invisible cap, come down in any town he pleased, slip into one shop or another and help himself to whatever his heart desired. After that he would get back on his flying carpet and fly on again. Some time passed, and he came to a hut that looked just like the first one. He stepped inside, and whom should he see there but another *Baba-Yaga the Leg of Stone, a very, very old and toothless crone.* "Greetings to you, Grandma!" said the soldier. "Do you know where I am to find my beautiful princess?" "No, my man, I don't. Go beyond so many seas and so many lands to where my elder sister lives, and perhaps she will be able to help you." "You're as old as old can be, you have lost all your teeth, but you know nothing that's of any use to anyone," the soldier said. And with these words he got on his flying carpet and flew off to see Baba-Yaga's elder sister.

He travelled for a long, long time, saw many lands and many seas, and at long last came to the end of the earth. A little hut stood there, with no road beyond it, but only darkness so deep that the eye could not pierce it. "If I do not find out what I want to know here, there will be nowhere else for me to go," said he to himself. He stepped into the hut, and whom should he see there but *Baba-Yaga the Leg of Stone, a very, very old and toothless crone.* "Greetings to you, Grandma! Tell me where I am to seek my beautiful princess," he said. "Wait!" said Baba-Yaga. "I will summon all my winds here and ask them about it. They travel all over the world, so they should know where she is." She stepped out onto the porch, gave a loud cry and a loud whistle, and from all sides rose winds so fierce that the hut began trembling and shaking. "Do not blow so hard, O wild winds!" Baba-Yaga cried. They gathered round her, and she said: "You have been blowing all over the world, so surely you can tell me where the beautiful princess is!" "We have not seen her," the winds replied with one voice. "But are all of you here?" "All save the south wind, Grandma."

Some little time passed, and the south wind came flying up. "Where have you been?" Baba-Yaga asked him. "I thought you would never come!" "Forgive me, Grandma!" the south wind said. "I was held up because I happened to find myself in a new kingdom where lives a most beautiful princess. She lost her husband, who vanished without a trace, and now many tsars, kings and princes are there pleading for her hand." "How far is it to this new kingdom?" Baba-Yaga asked. "It would take a man on foot thirty years and a man with wings ten years to get there, but I can carry him there in three hours." At this the soldier began begging the south wind with tears in his eyes to take him to the new kingdom. "Well, and why not!" the south wind said. "But before I do that you must promise to let me make merry there for three days and three nights." "I don't mind if you make merry there for three weeks!" "Very well, then. I'll take a little rest, and as soon as I feel that I'm strong enough for the journey we'll start on our way."

The south wind rested, and, when he had got back his strength, said to the soldier: "Well, my brave man, get ready, for we shall be starting off! Fear nothing, for no harm will come to you." And lo!—the wind began blowing and whistling, and it caught up the soldier and bore him to the very clouds. They sped over seas and mountains, and when only three hours had passed the soldier found himself in the new kingdom where lived his beautiful princess. "Farewell, my brave man," said the south wind. "I wish you well, so I will not blow or make merry in your kingdom." "And why not?" "Because if I do not a house will be left standing nor a tree growing in the whole of it!" "Goodbye, then, and many thanks to you," said the soldier, and, putting on his invisible cap, he made for the castle.

Now, as long as he was away not a tree was there in the garden but had withered, but as soon as he was back they came to life and burst into bloom. He stepped into a large chamber, and there, sitting round the table and drinking sweet wines, were the many tsars, kings and princes who had come to woo the princess. The soldier watched them, and as soon as anyone of them filled his glass and carried it to his lips he would knock the glass from his hand. And of all those present there none could understand why this was save the beautiful princess. "That must be my own dear husband come back to me," she told herself.

She glanced out of the window, and, seeing that the trees were all in bloom again, said: "Listen to me, all! I will tell you a little story and I will marry whichever of you can explain what it means. Here it is. There was once a box with a golden key. The key was lost, and I thought I would never see it again, but it has only just come back to me of itself. Now, what is that box and what is that key?" The tsars, kings and princes thought and pondered, but wise as they were and rack their brains as they might, they could not find the answer. "Show yourself to me, my own dear love!'' the princess said. The soldier took off his invisible cap, and, taking the princess's snow-white hands in his, kissed her on her sugar-sweet lips. ''Here is your answer!'' said the princess. ''It is I who am that box and it is my husband who is the golden key.'' After that there was nothing for the tsars, kings and princes to do but to leave the castle and turn their way homewards. And as for the princess and her husband, they lived happily together ever after. *They knew good health and they knew good cheer, and they prospered the more from year to year.*

Translated by Irina Zheleznova

The Princesses
Who Danced
the Nights Away

There once lived a king, a widower, who had twelve daughters, each more beautiful than the other. Every night the princesses would go off none knew where and they each of them wore out a pair of shoes every time. It was all the king could do to have enough shoes made for them, so he told himself that he must find out where his daughters went and what they did. With this in mind he held a feast, to which he invited kings, princes, nobles, merchants and commoners from many different lands, and he asked them to try to find out where his daughters went every night. And to him who would succeed he promised to give his favourite daughter in marriage and half his kingdom besides.

At first no one there would take up the challenge, but then a poor nobleman rose to his feet.

"I will try to find out where the princesses go, Your Majesty," said he.

The king was delighted, but the nobleman soon thought better of what he had done.

"Fool that I am!" said he to himself. "I know nothing about it, and if I don't find out quickly where the princesses go the king will have me thrown in jail."

He left the palace very sad and woebegone and walked straight on till he

found himself out of town, in the open country. By and by, coming toward him, he met an old woman who asked him why he looked so miserable.

"How can I help it!" the nobleman said. "I took it upon myself to find out where the king's daughters go every night, and I do not know how I am to do it."

"It's not easy, true," the old woman said, "but it's possible all the same! Here is an invisible cap for you—that is something that should help you—and remember this: when you go to bed the princesses will give you a sleeping potion to drink. Now, you must on no account drink it. Instead, you must turn to the wall and pour it out."

The nobleman thanked the old woman and went back to the palace.

Night was drawing on, and he was taken to a chamber next to the one the princesses slept in. He lay down on the bed and told himself that he would keep awake whatever happened. By and by one of the princesses brought him a cup of wine into which she had added some sleeping drops and begged him to drink it.

"Drink to me, brave youth!" said she.

The nobleman did not like to refuse, so he took the cup from her, but remembering what the old woman had told him, turned to the wall and poured out the wine.

Midnight struck, the princesses came to take a look at him, and the nobleman, who kept his ears open to catch every sound, pretended to be asleep.

"Well, sisters, our guard is asleep, so it's time for us to be off!" one of the princesses said.

"Yes, high time!" they all cried.

They put on the best of their finery, and then the eldest sister went up to her bed and moved it aside, revealing a steep staircase. This led down to a long passage which ran all the way to the cursed king's underworld kingdom. The princesses began climbing down the staircase one after another, and the nobleman got quickly out of bed, put on his invisible cap and went after them. He stepped on the hem of the youngest princess's dress, and she was frightened and said to her sisters:

"Someone seems to have stepped on my dress, sisters, and we may fare badly, for it's a bad sign."

"Don't be silly!" said they. "Nothing will happen."

They climbed down the staircase, went through the passage and found themselves in a grove where grew bushes abloom with golden flowers. The nobleman broke off a branch, and the whole grove swayed and rustled.

"Do you hear the grove rustling? That is a bad sign, sisters!" said the youngest princess.

"Never fear," said they. "It's only the sound of the music coming from the cursed king's palace."

They came to the palace and were met by the king and his courtiers. Music began playing, the princesses began to dance, and they did not stop till their shoes were quite worn out. Then the king bade the courtiers pour the wine and offer it to his guests, and the nobleman drank a glassful and slipped the glass in his pocket. The dance over, the princesses bade their partners goodbye and promised to be back again on the following night. They went home, undressed and were soon in bed and asleep.

Morning came, and the king had the poor nobleman summoned into his presence.

"Well, have you found out where my daughters go?" he asked.

"I have, Your Majesty!"

"Out with it, then!"

"They go to the cursed king's underworld kingdom and they spend the whole night long dancing."

The king called his daughters and asked them where they had spent the past night.

"We never left the palace!" said they.

"So you deny that you were in the cursed king's palace! This nobleman here says that that was where you were."

"How can he say such a thing, Father, when he slept the sleep of the dead all night!"

At this the nobleman drew a glass and a golden flower out of his pocket.

"Here's my proof!" said he.

It could not be helped, so the princesses confessed that they had indeed been in the cursed king's palace. The king then had the passage to the underground kingdom filled up with earth and sealed, and he gave his youngest daughter in marriage to the nobleman. And they all lived happily ever after *and never felt low or knew any woe.*

Translated by Irina Zheleznova

Bad Luck
and Good Luck

There once lived a peasant who had two sons. The peasant died, his sons decided to marry, and marry they did, the elder taking a poor girl to wife, and the younger, a rich one. They went on living in the same house, and it was not long before their wives began quarrelling.

Said the poor wife: "I married the elder brother, so I'm the one who should be mistress here."

Said the rich one: "No, not you, but I, for I am richer than you."

The brothers did nothing about it for a time, but, seeing that their wives went on quarrelling, divided up all that their father had left them between themselves and parted ways. The elder brother's family grew, for not a year passed but his wife had a child born to her, but with his farm things went from bad to worse and one day he found himself ruined. While there was money and bread in the house he had taken joy in his children, but when these were gone, all joy left him. There was nothing to be done, so he went to see his younger brother and begged him to help him. But the younger brother said that he had children of his own to look after and that he, the elder brother, was to live as best he could.

Some time passed, and the poor brother came to see the rich one again.

"Do please lend me your horse if only for a day," said he. "For how can I plough without one!"

"Oh, all right," said the younger brother. "Go to the field and take one of

91

my horses. But don't work it to death, mind!"

The poor brother came to the field and he saw a man, a stranger, ploughing there, his brother's horses pulling the plough.

"Stop!" he cried. "Tell me who you are."

"Who are you that you ask me this?" the stranger said.

"I ask you this because my brother's horses are pulling the plough."

"Can't you see that I'm your brother's Good Luck? He drinks and makes merry and knows not a care in the world, and I work for him."

"Where is my Good Luck, then?"

"Your Good Luck is lying under that bush yonder, and he does nothing but sleep day and night."

"Can that be so?" said the poor brother, and he added under his breath: "If it is, then I'll show you what's what, Good Luck of mine!"

He got himself a thick stick, crept up to his Good Luck and struck him with it with all his might. Good Luck started up in alarm.

"Why did you hit me?" he asked.

"Don't you know? I'll give you a thrashing you won't forget if you lie there and sleep while you should be busy ploughing like other people."

"You mean you want me to plough instead of you? I'll never do it, never!"

"Are you going to lie under that bush all the time, then? Why, I'll starve to death if you do."

"If you want me to help you, then give up farming and take up trade. I'm not used to farm work, but bying and selling is just in my line."

"Go in for trade indeed! How'll I start? I haven't a penny, I have nothing to eat even."

"Well, take your wife's old dress and sell it, and then buy a new one with the money you get and sell that. I'll be right there beside you, helping you."

"Oh, all right, then."

Morning came, and the poor man said to his wife:

"Get ready, wife, for we'll be moving to town."

"Whatever for?" the wife asked.

"I'm giving up farming and taking up trade."

"You must be mad! We have nothing to feed the children with even."

"What do you know about it! Pack our things, take the children, and we'll be off."

They packed their things, said a prayer, and were just about to lock the door when they heard someone inside the house weeping bitterly.

"Who is that weeping?" the poor brother called.

"It's me, your Bad Luck!" a voice called back.

"What are you crying about?"

"How can I help it! You are going away and leaving me here."

"Don't you think it! I'll take you with me, that's what I'll do. Hey, wife! Empty one of the chests, will you?"

The wife did as he asked.

"Come, Bad Luck, get into the chest!" the poor brother said.

Bad Luck did as he said, and the poor brother at once slammed the lid shut

and locked the chest. Then he dug a hole in the ground, buried the chest in it and said:

"A curse on you, Bad Luck, may you stay there forever, I hope I never see you again!"

He came to town with his wife and children, rented a room for them to live in and started trading. He took his wife's old dress to market and sold it for a rouble, and then he bought a new dress for the money and sold it for two roubles. Luck went his way, so that he got a double price for whatever it was he sold, and he was soon rich enough to join a merchant's guild. Hearing about it, his younger brother came to see him.

"How did you manage to grow rich so quickly?" asked he.

"It was simple," said the elder brother. "I locked up my Bad Luck in a chest and buried the chest."

"Where did you bury it?"

"In the yard of my house in the village."

Now, this filled the younger brother with such envy that the tears came to his eyes. He rode to the village, dug up the chest and let Bad Luck out of it.

"Go join my brother and ruin him," said he.

"Oh no!" Bad Luck said. "I'd rather stay with you. That villain of a brother of yours all but killed me, and you let me out!"

He did as he said and stayed with the rich brother, and the rich brother soon became very, very poor.

Translated by Irina Zheleznova

The Early Match

There were once two rich merchants, one living in Moscow and one in Kiev. They often met on matters of business, were good friends and never failed to share whatever food and drink they had with them. One day the Kiev merchant came to Moscow, and, meeting his friend, said: "I have been blessed by God, my wife has given birth to a son." "And mine to a daughter," said the Moscow merchant. "Good! Let's strike a bargain! I have a son, you a daughter, so why not have them marry when they grow up. Then we'll not only be friends but relations too!" "Very well, only it's not that simple. Why, for all you and I know, your son might refuse to marry my daughter. The only way is for you to give me twenty thousand roubles as a pledge of your good faith." "But what if your daughter should die?" "Then you'll get your money back." No more was said, and the Kiev merchant brought out twenty thousand roubles and handed them to the Moscow merchant who pocketed them and went home. "I have promised our daughter in marriage to the son of a friend of mine," said he to his wife. The wife was quite taken aback. "Are you mad?" said she. "Why, she's only a babe in arms." "What of that! I even got twenty thousand roubles as a pledge of my friend's good faith," the merchant said.

What's done is done, and the two merchants went on living each in his own town and never paid one another a visit: the distance was great, for one thing, and their businesses kept them at home, for another. Meanwhile their children grew, and if the son was good to look at, the daughter was even more so. Eigh-

teen years passed, and the Moscow merchant, never having heard from his Kiev friend, promised his daughter in marriage to a colonel. Now, it was at this same time that the Kiev merchant called his son and said to him: "You are to go to Moscow, my son. There is a lake there where I once set a trap for a duck. Now, if a duck has been caught in the trap, then bring the duck here; but if none has, then bring back the trap." The son got ready and set out for Moscow. On and on he rode, and there was only a last stretch of road left when he came to a river. The river was spanned by a wooden bridge, but the bridge had been left unfinished and only the half nearest to him was boarded over.

Now, the colonel too happened to be travelling along the selfsame road. He drove up to the bridge, and not knowing how he was to get to the opposite bank, stopped his coach. He saw the merchant's son and asked him where he was going and why. "I am going to Moscow," the merchant's son replied. "There is a lake there on which my father set a trap these eighteen years ago, and he now wants me to see if a duck has been caught in it. If it has, then I am to take the duck to him; if not, then I am to bring back the trap." "How strange!" said the colonel to himself. "A trap can hardly last for eighteen years. And even if it can, what about the duck—surely a duck does not live that long!" He thought and he thought about it, but the whole thing seemed as strange to him as before and he could not make head or tail of it. "How are we going to cross the river?" asked he. "Get into my coach, and you'll see," said the merchant's son. He urged on his horses, and when he came to the middle of the bridge, climbed out of the coach and went back on foot. He removed the first of the boards from the bridge, carried them to where he had left his coach, and, having nailed them to the end boards, was able to move the coach ahead a little. This he repeated over and over again till the coach was safely across the bridge. After that he and the colonel rode on till they reached Moscow. "Where are you going to put up?" the colonel asked. "In the house where spring meets winter on the gate," the merchant's son told him. They took leave of one another and went their separate ways.

The merchant's son found lodgings in the house of an old woman, and the colonel rushed off to see his bride. He was treated royally by her mother and father who gave him food and drink and asked him if he had had a good journey. He told them about the man he had met, a merchant's son, and of how he had asked him where he was going and was told that he was going to Moscow to try and bring back to his father either the trap he had set eighteen years ago or a duck, if one had been caught in the trap. "Now, it was then that we had to cross the river," the colonel went on, "and this was no easy matter as only one half of the bridge spanning it had been boarded over. I did not know what to do, but the merchant's son, clever lad that he is, did. He crossed the bridge, and he took me across with him." "Where has this man put up?" the bride asked. "In the house where spring meets winter on the gate, to use his own words," the colonel said.

The merchant's daughter ran to her room. "Take a jug of milk, a loaf of bread and a basket of eggs," said she to her maidservant. "Drink some of the milk, eat a bit of the bread and an egg, and then go to the house where some

97

grass and some hay is tied to the gate. Find the Kiev merchant's son there, give him the milk, bread and eggs and ask him, first, whether the level of the sea has risen or fallen, second, whether there is a full moon or a half-moon in the sky, and third, whether all of the stars are out." The maidservant did as she was told. She found the Kiev merchant's son, gave him the milk, the bread and the eggs and said: "I am going to ask you three questions and you must answer them. Here is the first: Has the level of the sea risen or fallen?" "It has fallen," said the merchant's son. "Here's my second question," the maidservant said. "Is there a full moon or a half-moon in the sky?" "A half-moon." "And now here's my third question: are all the stars out?" "Not all, one is missing," said the merchant's son. The maidservant went back to her mistress and passed on to her the merchant son's replies. Said the merchant's daughter to her father: "I cannot marry the colonel, Father, for I have a fiancé already who misses me sadly. And it was you who struck a bargain with his father and promised me to him." The merchant's son was at once sent for, he and the merchant's daughter were married, and a feast was held to celebrate the wedding. And as for the colonel he was sent away with nothing to show for it.

Now, I was at that wedding too. *I drank mead and I drank wine, and all of it ran down this beard of mine* and none got into my mouth.

Translated by Irina Zheleznova

Lutonya

There once lived an old man and an old woman who had a son named Lutonya. One day the father and son were busy doing something in the yard when they heard the old woman, who was in the house, give a loud scream. The old man hurried into the house, and, seeing the old woman in tears, asked her what had happened. "Well it was like this, old man," said she. "I wanted to make up a fire, so I picked up a log, but I dropped it before ever I got it into the oven. So I said to myself I said, 'Now what if Lutonya were married and had a son and that son were sitting just in front of the oven, why, the log might have fallen on him and killed him!'" And she began weeping again. At this the old man's eyes too filled with tears, and his moans and wails were as loud as any uttered by his wife. "It's true, old woman, you might indeed have killed him!" he cried.

Hearing them, Lutonya came running into the house. "What are you two crying about?" he asked. "Why," said they, "had you been married and had had a son and that son had been sitting here a while back, the log the old woman dropped might have fallen on him and killed him!"

Lutonya picked up his hat. "Goodbye!" he said. "If I find anyone more foolish than you, then I'll come back. If not, I won't, and you needn't wait for me." And with these words he left the house and went away.

On and on he walked and he saw some men dragging a cow up on to the roof of a house. "Why are you dragging the cow up on to the roof for?"

99

Lutonya asked. "Can't you see? Because there's grass growing there, that's why!" "The more fools you!" said Lutonya. He climbed up on to the roof of the house, picked the grass and threw it down to the cow. The men were both surprised and pleased at this and they begged Lutonya to stay with them and teach them wisdom. "No," said Lutonya, "I can't do that. There are many other fools in the world, and I have yet to meet them." And on he went.

By and by he came to a village and saw a crowd of men beating a horse with sticks in order to force it to fit its head into a yoke they had hung over a gate. And though the horse could hardly stand it was so weary they never stopped. "What are you doing?" Lutonya asked. "Can't you see? We're trying to harness the horse!" they said. "The more fools you! Here, let me do it." And he lifted the yoke off the gate and put it round the horse's neck. And these men too were filled with wonder that anyone should be so clever and begged Lutonya to stay with them for at least a week and teach them wisdom. But Lutonya would not listen to them and went on.

He walked and he walked, and by and by, feeling tired, turned into an inn. And great was his surprise when he saw the owner of the inn, an old woman, running out of the house and back in again, a spoon in her hand. She had cooked her sons some oat jelly, and, having placed it on the table, kept going to the cellar for a spoonful of sour-cream. "Why should you wear your shoes out for no good reason, old woman?" Lutonya asked. "No good reason, you say?" the old woman replied. "Can't you see that the jelly is in the house and the sour-cream in the cellar?" "Well, why don't you bring the jug of sour-cream here instead of running back and forth like this? It would make things much easier." "You're right, good youth, you're right!" She brought the jug of sour-cream into the house and invited Lutonya to sit beside her and try some of her jelly. Lutonya ate till he could eat no more, and then he climbed up on to a big shelf over the stove that was used for a bed, and fell fast asleep. And as soon as he wakes, *I'll go on without fail with the rest of my tale.*

Translated by Irina Zheleznova

The Snake Princess

One day a Cossack who was riding his horse happened to stray off the road and found himself in a small glade deep in a dense forest. There was a haystack in the middle of the glade, and the Cossack, who was tired, lay down beside it and lit his pipe. He lay there smoking and never noticed that a spark from his pipe had dropped on to the hay. After a while, feeling rested, he got on his horse and started on his way, but he was no more than a dozen paces or so from the haystack when the hay burst into flame. The whole forest was lit up, and the Cossack looked back and saw that the haystack was now a ball of fire and that amid the flames stood a lovely young maid. "Save me, Cossack, please save me!" the maid called out. "I would if I could reach you," the Cossack said. "But I can't, there's flame all around you." "Thrust your lance into the flame, and I will climb on to it and out." The Cossack did as she said and himself turned away, for the heat was such that it could not be borne.

And lo!—the maid turned into a snake, crawled up on to the lance and along it on to the Cossack's neck, wound herself thrice round it and took her tail between her teeth. The Cossack was frightened, but the snake said in a human voice: "Have no fear, brave youth! Carry me round on your neck for seven years and seek the tin kingdom, and as soon as you find it stay there for another seven years without ever leaving it. If you succeed in doing this, you will find true happiness!"

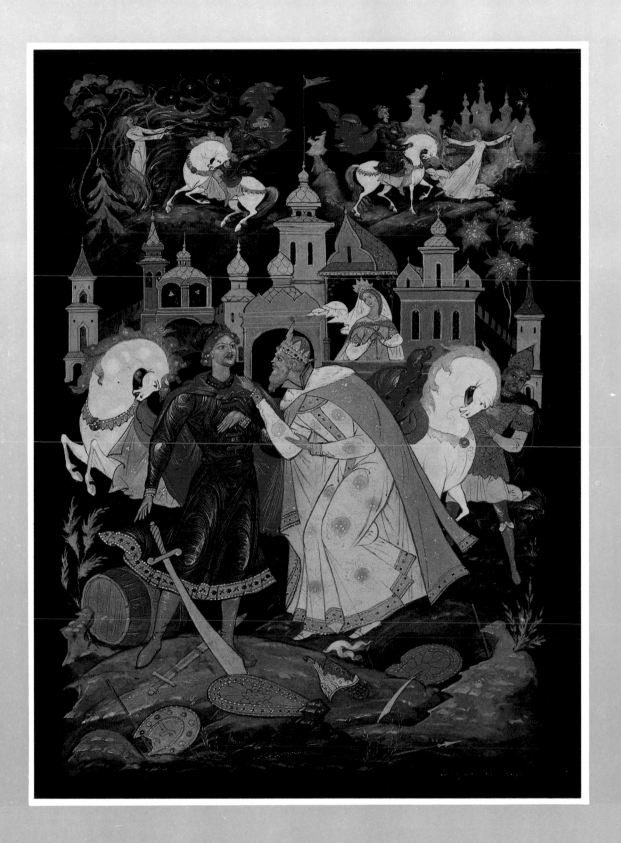

The Cossack set off to seek the tin kingdom. He travelled for a long, long time, but it was not till seven years had passed that he reached a steep mountain, on top of which stood a tin castle surrounded by a high wall of white stone. He galloped up the mountain, reached the wall, which slid open before him, and rode into a wide courtyard. And the same moment the snake tore herself from his neck, struck the ground, and, turning into a lovely young maid again, vanished. The Cossack put his trusty horse in a stable, came into the castle and began going from room to room and looking them over. There were mirrors everywhere, and things made of silver, and cushions and hangings of velvet, but not a soul was there in sight. "What a strange place this is!" said the Cossack to himself. "There is no one here to offer me food or drink. I'm afraid I'll starve to death!" He looked up, and there before him he saw a table groaning with food and drink. The Cossack ate and drank, and, feeling much better, decided to go and take a look at his horse. He came into the stable, and there was the horse standing in a stall and filling itself up on oats. "Good! Very good!" the Cossack told himself. "There's nothing to worry about, I see, one can lead a life of ease here."

But the months passed into years, and the Cossack, who never left the tin castle, was bored to distraction. For always to be alone and not have anyone to exchange a word with was not at all easy! So unhappy did he at last begin to feel that the day came when he drank till he was quite drunk. Then it was that he decided to leave the castle, but no matter where he went, high walls rose up before him and he could not pass through them. At last, so vexed was he by this that he seized a stick and began smashing the mirrors, ripping the cushions, breaking the chairs and throwing the silver knickknacks about. And all the while he kept hoping that the master of the castle would come and set him free. But no one appeared, and the Cossack went to bed and to sleep. It was morning when he woke, and after taking a walk round the castle, began to feel very hungry. But though he looked here and he looked there, he found not so much as a crust of bread. "I have only myself to blame," said he to himself. "If I hadn't behaved the way I did yesterday, I wouldn't be going hungry today." And no sooner had he said this than food and drink appeared before him!

Three days passed, and it was on the morning of the fourth day, when the Cossack woke and looked out of the window, that he saw his horse, saddled, waiting by the porch. What could it mean? He washed, dressed, said his prayers, and, taking his lance, stepped outside, and lo and behold!—as if out of thin air the Snake Princess appeared before him. "Good morrow, good youth!" said she. "The seven years are up, you have saved my life, and I thank you from the bottom of my heart. Know this: I am the daughter of a king and was carried off from my parents' house by Koshchei the Deathless. Koshchei was in love with me and wanted to marry me, and it was because I would not have him and only mocked at him that he turned me into a snake. And now let us go to my father. He will want to reward you and will offer you gold and precious gems, but you must not accept them. Ask him instead for the barrel that stands in the palace

104

cellar." "What good will the barrel do me?" "It is a magic barrel. Roll it to the right of you, and a palace will appear before you; roll it to the left of you, and the palace will vanish." "Very well, I will do as you say," said the Cossack. He mounted his horse, put the Snake Princess in front of him on the horse's back, and, the castle walls sliding open before them, set out on his way.

Whether a short time passed or a long nobody knows, but he came at last to the kingdom of the Snake Princess's father. The king was overjoyed to see his daughter, he thanked the Cossack over and over again and placed sacks full of gold and pearls before him. "I have no need of gold or of pearls," said the Cossack. "Just let me have the barrel standing in your cellar." "You ask for much too much, Cossack," said the king. "But as my daughter is more precious to me than anything in the world, you can have the barrel. Take it and God be with you." He had the barrel brought in, and the Cossack took it and set out to see the world.

On and on he rode, and he met a very old man coming toward him. "Do give me something to eat, good youth!" the old man begged. The Cossack at once jumped off his horse. He undid the rope with which the barrel was tied to the saddle and rolled the barrel to the right of him, and lo!—a rich palace appeared before him. He and the old man stepped inside, and they found themselves in a chamber with beautifully painted walls. A table covered with a white cloth stood before them. They sat down at it, and the Cossack called for food and drink. "Come, my faithful servants!" he cried. "Make haste, for my guest is hungry!" And no sooner were the words out of his mouth than the servants came in bearing a whole roast ox and three barrels of beer. The old man lay to with gusto and he praised the food and drink in loud tones. He ate up the whole of the ox and drained all the three barrels of beer, grunted and said: "I could have done with more, but thank you all the same, for it's a kind and a generous host you've been to me."

They left the palace, the Cossack rolled the barrel to the left of him, and the palace vanished. "Let's trade," said the old man. "You give me your barrel, and I'll give you my sword." "What good is the sword to me?" the Cossack asked. "It's a sword that smites of itself. All you have to do is wave it, and even if there should be a numberless host before you, it will hack every last man of it to pieces. Do you see that forest? I'll show you what my sword is worth." He brought out the sword, waved it and said: "Come, sword-smites-of-itself, cut down that forest yonder!" And away the sword flew and began cutting down the trees, and it was only when it had brought down the whole of the forest that it came back to its master. The Cossack never stopped to think. He gave the old man his barrel and took his sword in exchange, and then he waved the sword and killed the old man on the spot. After that, the barrel being his again, he tied it to the saddle, and, mounting his horse, set out for the Snake Princess's kingdom. Now, the capital of the kingdom had been laid siege to by foes, and as the Cossack was nearing it he saw a numberless host at its walls. He waved his sword and said "Come, sword-smites-of-itself, do me a service, cut down the

105

whole of the enemy host!" and at once heads began to fly and blood to flow, and before an hour had passed the whole of the battlefield was strewn with the bodies of the dead.

The king rode out to meet the Cossack. He embraced him warmly and said that he could have his daughter in marriage if he wished. The Cossack and the Snake Princess were married, and the wedding feast was as rich as any that was ever held. *I was there, I drank mead and wine, and all of it ran down this beard of mine.*

Translated by Irina Zheleznova

The Wonder
of Wonders

Once upon a time there lived a rich merchant and his wife. The merchant traded in rare wares, and not a year passed but he would go travelling to foreign parts. One day he had a ship fitted out and began preparing for a voyage, and he asked his wife what it was she wanted him to bring her for a present. "I have enough of everything," said she. "But if you want to please me, bring me the wonder of wonders." "Very well, I will try to find it," the merchant said.

Off he sailed beyond the thrice-nine lands, and, coming to a rich city, sold all of his wares there and loaded his ship with new ones. This done, he went for a walk, and as he strolled along the streets he asked himself where it was he could find the wonder of wonders. By and by, coming toward him, he met an old man, a stranger, who asked him why he looked so sad. "How can I help it!" the merchant said. "I want to buy the wonder of wonders for my wife, but I do not know where it is to be found." "Why didn't you say so in the first place!" the old man said. "The wonder of wonders is something I have at home, and I will sell it to you since you seem to want it so badly."

They went along together, and the old man brought the merchant to his house. "Do you see that goose there walking in the yard?" the old man asked. "Yes. What of it?" "Well, then, watch and see what will happen to it," said the old man, and he called in a loud voice: "Come inside, goose!" The goose waddled into the house, and the old man picked up a frying pan. "Come, goose, lie down on the frying pan!" said he. The goose did as it was told, and the old

107

man put the frying pan into the oven, roasted the goose and, when it was ready, placed it on the table. "Come, my good man," said he, "move up a chair and let us eat. Only mind, do not throw any of the bones under the table but gather them all in a heap." They polished off the goose, and the old man took the bones, and, wrapping them in a cloth, threw them on the floor. "Come, goose, shake out your feathers and go out into the yard!" he cried. And lo!—the goose rose, shook out its feathers and waddled off into the yard, and it was as if it had never been in the oven at all. "Now, that is really the wonder of wonders you have there, old man!" said the merchant. They struck a bargain, the merchant paid the old man a big sum of money for the goose, and, taking it on board ship, set sail for his homeland.

Once there, he greeted his wife, and, giving her the goose, told her that it could be roasted as many times as she liked, but would come to life again every time.

They went to bed and to sleep, and on the following day, the merchant had no sooner gone off to his shop than his wife's lover came running to pay her a visit. She was more than pleased to see him, and, wanting to treat him to some roast goose, leaned out of the window and called: "Come here, goose!" The goose came waddling into the house. "Come, goose, lie down on the frying pan!" said she. But the goose made no move to do this, and so angry did it make the merchant's wife that she struck it with an iron pan holder. The same moment the holder's one end stuck to the goose, and the other to her, and try as she would she could not tear it off. "Oh! Oh!" she cried, and she begged her lover to help her. The lover threw both his arms round her and pulled hard, but instead of tearing her from the pan holder, only got stuck to her himself.

The goose waddled out into the street, and, dragging the two of them after him, made for the merchant's shop. The tradesmen saw them and began trying to tear them apart, but with no better success, for whoever so much as touched them got stuck to them in his turn. The townsfolk came running to watch and marvel, and, hearing the noise, the merchant stepped out of his shop to see what the commotion was all about. The sight of his wife and of the men, who seemed to be holding on to her fast, struck him as suspicious. "Come, confess your sins!" said he to her. "For if you don't, you'll stay stuck to the goose forever!" It could not be helped, and the merchant's wife told her husband all about everything and begged him to forgive her. The merchant tore her away from her lover, gave the lover a sound trouncing and then led his wife home where he went at her with his fists, saying every time he struck her: "Take that, wife! Here's the wonder of wonders for you!"

Translated by Irina Zheleznova

The Seven Simeons

In a certain village there was once a peasant who had seven sons all named Simeon. They were tall and comely youths enough, each more handsome than the other, but so lazy and shiftless that it would not have been easy to find their match anywhere. They refused to do anything at all, and their father had such a hard time with them that he decided to take them to the king and ask him to take them into his service. This he did, and the king thanked him for bringing him such fine-looking young men and asked what they could do. "Ask them yourself, Your Majesty!" the peasant said. The king had the eldest of the Simeons come up to him first. "Is there anything you know how to do?" he asked him. "I know how to rob and to steal, Your Majesty," Simeon replied. "Good! I may yet have need of you," the king said. He then called the second of the Simeons and asked him what he could do. "I can make all sorts of beautiful things of iron and other metals," the second Simeon told him. "I may well have need of you too," the king said. And so it went. The third of the Simeons told the king that he could shoot birds in flight, the fourth that he could retrieve felled birds the way dogs do, the fifth, that if he placed himself in a high enough spot he could see what went on in all of the kingdoms of the world, the sixth, that he could build a ship at a single blow of his axe, and the seventh, that he could treat and cure the sick.

Time passed, and, one day the king decided to marry a certain princess. He turned over in his mind whom to send after her and thought of the seven

110

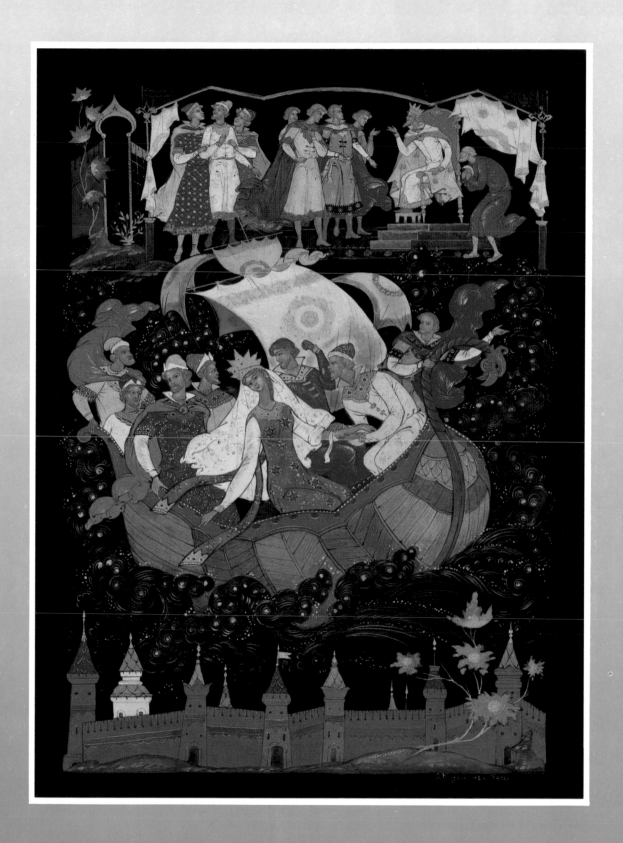

Simeons. He had them summoned to the palace, bade them bring the princess to him and gave them a large number of soldiers for an escort.

The seven Simeons were soon ready to be on their way, and the sixth of them having built a ship with one blow of his axe, they at once set sail.

They reached the kingdom where the princess lived, and the fifth of them climbed a mast and said that the princess was alone in her chamber and could be easily carried off. The second of the Simeons forged many beautiful things, and he and the first of the Simeons or Simeon the Robber went to the palace together to sell them. This, however, was only a pretext, for they were no sooner in the palace than Simeon the Robber seized the princess and carried her off.

What they had set out to do accomplished, the seven Simeons set sail for home, but the princess turned herself into a white swan and flew away. At this the third of the Simeons, who was a fine shot, wasted no time but snatched a rifle and shot her through her left wing. The swan fell into the water, but the fourth of the Simeons jumped overboard, and, snatching her up, brought her back on board. The swan then turned into a princess again, but when it was found that she could not move her arm, the seventh of the Simeons, the one who could cure the sick, treated her wound and made her well again.

The seven Simeons came back to their kingdom in good health and spirits, and they fired a cannon to let the king know of their arrival. Now, so much time had passed since they had left on their voyage that the king had forgotten all about them, and he now commanded his servants to go and find out whose ship it was that had sailed into view. The servants did as they were bade, and then told the king that the seven Simeons were back and had brought with them the princess he wanted to wed. The king was quite overwhelmed by such prowess, and he ordered that drums be beaten and cannon fired in their honour. But when the princess saw the king she said that he was too old for her and refused to marry him. "Whom then, do you wish to marry, fair maiden?" the king asked her. "Him who carried me off from the palace," said the princess. Now, Simeon the Robber was a dashing young man, and it was not to be wondered at that he had caught the princess's fancy. And as for the king, he was secretly relieved and ordered that they be wed without another word. After that, saying that it was time for him to give up his throne and rest, he made Simeon the Robber king in his stead, and all of his six brothers, great nobles.

Translated by Irina Zheleznova

The Birch-Tree
and the Three Falcons

There was once a soldier who served out his term in the army and was then retired. He decided to go home, and as he was on his way there he met the evil spirit coming toward him. "Stop, soldier! Where are you going?" asked the evil spirit. "Home!" the soldier replied. "Why should you go home?" said the evil spirit. "You have no kith or kin and nothing in the world you can call your own. Better take up service with me, I will pay you a good salary." "What will I have to do?" the soldier asked. "Nothing very hard, believe me. I am about to set out beyond the blue seas to attend my daughter's wedding and will be leaving my three falcons behind. What you will have to do is watch over them until I return." The soldier thought this over. "What is life without money!" said he to himself. "This way I'll earn something at least even if I'll only be working for the devil!" They struck a bargain, and the evil spirit took the soldier to his house and himself flew away beyond the blue seas.

The soldier began walking from room to room for want of anything better to do, and this bored him so much that he went out for a stroll in the garden. And the first thing he saw there was a birch-tree which said to him in a human voice: "Please, soldier, go to such-and-such a village and ask the village priest to give you that which he saw in a dream this past night." The soldier did as the birch-tree said, and the priest at once brought out a book. "Here, take this book!" said he. The soldier took it and went back to the birch-tree. "Thank you, my good man!" said the birch-tree. "And now stand here beside me and read!"

113

The soldier began to read the book. He read for a night, and the head and neck of a maid fair beyond compare appeared from out of the birch-tree; he read for a second night, and nearly all of her did; he read for a third night, and out she stepped from the tree and kissed him. "I am the daughter of a king," said she. "The evil spirit carried me off and turned me into a birch-tree. And as for the three falcons, they are my own brothers who tried to free me and were caught themselves." And she no sooner finished speaking than the three falcons came flying up, struck the earth and turned into tall and handsome youths. Then the four of them got ready and started out for home, and they took the soldier with them.

The king and queen were overjoyed to see them. They rewarded the soldier richly and had him marry the princess and live in the palace with them.

Translated by Irina Zheleznova

The Magic Box

There was once a peasant and his wife who had a son old enough to learn a trade. The father did not know what to teach him, so he decided to apprentice him to a master. He went to town and agreed with the master that his son would stay with him for three years and only come home once at the end. Then he handed over his son. The boy lived there for a year, then another, and soon learnt to fashion fine things, even excelling the master himself. He made a clock worth five hundred roubles and sent it to his father. "Let him sell it," he thought, "and relieve his poverty." But how could the father sell it! He could not marvel enough at the fine clock which his own son had made. Soon it was time for the lad to visit his parents. Now his master was very strict and said:

"Off you go. You have three hours and three minutes. If you are not back by then, you shall pay with your life."

"How can I get to father's place in that time?" thought the lad.

"Take that carriage over there and close your eyes tight," replied the master.

The lad did as he was told. He closed his eyes tight and when he opened them, there he was at his father's house. He went inside and no one was there. His father and mother had seen the carriage draw up, taken fright and hidden in the cellar. He had a job persuading them to come out. They embraced and his mother wept because it had been such a long time. Their son had brought them presents. They were so busy talking that they did not notice the time until the

116

three hours were up and only three minutes remained. Then only one! The devil whispered to the lad:

"Make haste, or your master will show you..."

The lad took his leave properly and set off. Soon he arrived, went into the house and saw that the devil was tormenting his master because he was late. The lad plucked up his courage and fell at his master's feet:

"Forgive me for being late, I won't do it again."

His master let him off with a scolding and forgave him.

So the lad went on living there and began to make much finer things than anyone else. The master was afraid that if the lad left he would lose all his trade, for the boy was more skilled than him now. So he said to him:

"Hey, fellow. Go to the underworld and bring me a box from there. It's standing on the royal throne."

They sewed some leather thongs together and tied a little bell to each seam. The master began to lower the lad into a kind of ravine and told him that if he got the box he must shake the thongs, so the bells would ring and the master would hear. The lad descended into the underworld, saw a house and went inside. Some twenty men stood up and bowed before him, saying:

"Hail, Prince Ivan."

The lad was amazed at such honours. He went into another room, full of women. They too stood up and said:

"Hail, Prince Ivan!"

These people had been sent down there by the master. The lad went into the third room and saw a throne with a box on it. He took the box and bade the people follow him.

They came to the thong rope, shook it, tied one of the men to it and the master pulled him up. Prince Ivan wanted to wait until last with the box. The master pulled half the men out. Suddenly a workman ran up and called him home—there had been an accident. The master went off, having told them to pull everybody out of the underworld except the peasant's son. So they brought all the men up, but left the lad at the bottom. He wandered aimlessly around the underworld, until he happened to shake the box and suddenly out jumped twelve stalwart youths and said:

"What is your command, Prince Ivan?"

"Take me up out of here."

The stalwart youths took hold of him and carried him up. He went not to his master, but straight to his father. Meanwhile the master remembered about the magic box, ran to the ravine and shook the thong ladder hard, but the lad was not there. "He must have gone off somewhere! I'd better send someone after him," thought the master.

The peasant's son lived for a while with his father, then chose a good spot and tossed the box from one hand to the other. Suddenly the twenty-four stalwart youths appeared.

"What is your command, Prince Ivan?"

"Build a kingdom on this spot, fairer than any other kingdom."

The kingdom appeared! The lad settled there, got married and lived in

117

plenty. Now in that kingdom was a certain hefty fellow whose mother used to go to Prince Ivan to beg alms. One day her son said to her:

"Steal the king's box from him, Mother."

Prince Ivan was not at home. His wife gave the old woman alms and went out. The old woman grabbed the box, put it in a sack and went off to her son. He tossed the box from one hand to the other and out jumped the twenty-four stalwart youths. He ordered them to cast Prince Ivan into the deep pit for dead cattle and turn his wife and parents into servants. Then he himself became king.

The peasant's son sat at the bottom of the pit for three days, wondering how to get out. He saw a large bird carrying off the dead cattle. So he went and tied himself to a dead cow. The bird seized the cow, flew up and perched on a pine branch, with Prince Ivan dangling down, unable to untie himself. Suddenly a soldier appeared, took aim and fired his musket. The bird fluttered away, dropping the cow. The cow fell down with Prince Ivan tumbling after it. He untied himself and set off, wondering: "How am I going to get my kingdom back?" He felt in his pocket. There was the key to the box. He tossed it up. Suddenly two stalwart youths appeared.

"What is your command, Prince Ivan?"

"I'm in trouble, my good men."

"We know and you're lucky we stayed behind."

"Couldn't you bring me the box, lads?"

No sooner said than done. The two stalwart youths brought him the box. He came to life at once, ordered the old beggar woman and her son to be executed and began to rule the land as before.

Translated by K. M. Cook-Horujy

The Golden Shoe

Once upon a time there lived an old man and an old woman who had two daughters. One day the old man went to market and bought each of them a fish, one for the older daughter and one for the younger. The older daughter ate her fish, but the younger one took hers to a well and asked it whether she was to eat it or not. "Do not eat me but let me down into the water, for I may be of help to you some day," said the fish. The girl let the fish down into the well and herself went home.

Now, the old woman had never liked her younger daughter. One day she dressed the older daughter in the finest of clothes and prepared to go to church with her, but to the younger one she gave two measures of rye and bade her pick it out before they were back. The girl went to the well for water, she sat down by it and wept, and the fish she had set free swam up and asked her why she was crying. "How can I help it!" the girl replied. "My mother dressed my sister in the finest of clothes and went to church with her, but she left me at home and bade me pick out two measures of rye before she was back." "Do not cry but dress yourself in the best of finery and go to church too!" said the fish. "And as for the rye, it will all be picked out for you." The girl dressed herself in the best of finery and drove off to church, and she looked so beautiful that her mother, who saw her there, did not recognize her. The service was nearing its end when the girl left the church, and her mother came home soon after her. "Have you picked out the rye, you little silly?" asked she. "I have," said the girl. "There

120

was a most beautiful girl in church today!" the mother said. "The priest had eyes for none but her and could hardly chant his prayers or read his sermon because of it! And just take a look at yourself, you little silly, you're smutty and dirty and have nothing but rags on." "I wasn't there, but I know just how it was," said the girl. "Stop talking nonsense, how can you know anything of the kind!" said the mother.

Some time passed, and one day the mother dressed her older daughter in the finest of clothes again and went to church with her, but she left the younger one at home, bidding her pick out three measures of wheat and get it all done before they were back. The girl went to the well for water, she sat down by it and began to cry, and the fish swam up and asked her why she was crying. "How can I help it!" the girl replied. "My mother dressed my sister in the finest of clothes and went to church with her, but she left me at home and bade me pick out three measures of wheat before they were back." "Do not cry, fair maid!" said the fish. "Dress yourself in the best of finery and go to church too. And as for the wheat, it will all be picked out for you."

The girl dressed herself in the best of finery, came to church and began to pray. And the priest had eyes for none but her and could hardly chant his prayers or read his sermon because of it. Now, among the people attending the service there was a prince who fell in love with the girl at sight. He was bent on finding out who she was, and with this in mind, smeared the floor with tar. By then the service was nearly over, and the girl hurried to the door, but her shoe stuck to the tar, and she had to slip out of it and leave it, sewn with gold though it was, behind her. The prince found it and held it up for all to see. "I will marry her whose shoe this is!" said he.

The old woman came home and began singing the praises of the girl she had seen. "Never was there anyone so beautiful!" said she. "The priest had eyes for none but her and could hardly chant his prayers or read his sermon because of it. And look at you, you little silly, what a sight you are, all smutty and dirty and dressed in rags!"

Meanwhile, the prince had been searching for the girl who had lost her shoe, but the shoe was too small for all who tried it on, and though he went all over he could not find anyone it would fit. In due time he came to the old woman's house and asked her to have her younger daughter come out and try on the shoe to see if it fit her. "She will only get the shoe dirty!" said the old woman. But the girl came out, the prince had her try on the shoe, and lo!—it turned out to be a perfect fit. He and the girl were married, and *they lived together in good health and good cheer and prospered the more from year to year.*

Translated by Irina Zheleznova

Words of Wisdom

Once upon a time there lived a man named Ivan who was called Ivan the Luckless One because he never had any luck. No matter how hard he worked he was paid no more than twenty kopeks whereas another in his place might have got a ruble or even two. "Was I born different from other people that I should be treated so?" he asked himself. "I think I'll go to the king and ask him about it." He came to the palace and was ushered into the king's presence. "What brings you here, my good man?" asked the king. "Please, Your Majesty, do tell me why I never meet with any luck," Ivan said. The king called his nobles and generals and put the question to them, but though they all cudgeled their brains and thought very, very hard they could think of nothing. It was the princess who broke the silence. "Don't you think, Father," said she to the king, "that if Ivan were to find himself a wife, God might be kinder to him?" The king flew into a temper. "If you are as wise as all that and a better judge of things than any of us," cried he, "then you had better marry him yourself!" And the long and the short of it was that the princess and Ivan the Luckless One were married, and then the two of them were driven out of town so that their very names might be forgotten by all who had ever known them.

Ivan and the princess had nowhere else to go, so they came to the shore of the sea, and the princess said: "Well, husband, we are not here to reign over the land; what we must do is think how to make ends meet. So why don't you build us a little hut so that we can live in it and do our work and pray to God." Ivan

123

did as she said. He built a little hut, and he and his young wife settled in it. On the following day the princess gave him a kopek and told him to buy her some silk thread, and when he had done so and brought it to her she wove a beautiful rug out of it. "And now go and sell the rug, Ivan," said she. Off went Ivan with the rug, and he met an old man coming toward him. "Is that rug of yours for sale?" the old man asked. "Yes, indeed," Ivan replied. "How much do you want for it?" "A hundred rubles." "What good will it do you if I give you the money, you'll only lose it!" said the old man. "Better give me the rug and I will tell you a few words of wisdom in return." "I can't do that, old man," said Ivan. "I'm very poor and need money badly." The old man said nothing more. He counted out the one hundred rubles and gave them to Ivan, but when Ivan got home he found that he had lost the money on the way.

The princess, who had some thread left, made another rug, one even more beautiful, and Ivan set out to market to sell it, but as he was on his way there he again met the same old man. "How much do you want for your rug?" the old man asked. "Two hundred rubles." "What do you need the money for, you'll only lose it again! Why don't you let me have the rug, and I will tell you a few words of wisdom in return?" Ivan thought this over. "Oh, all right, let's hear your words of wisdom!" said he. "Here they are!" said the old man. "Never let your anger get the better of you." And he took the rug and went away. "What am I going to do now?" Ivan asked himself. "How can I show myself to my wife empty-handed! I had better go where the road leads."

He set out on his way, he walked and he walked, and he never stopped till he came to a far-off land. And he had only been there a short time when he heard that a twelve-headed dragon was eating up all who lived there. Now, Ivan was very tired, so he sat down by the wayside and began talking to himself, saying loudly: "He who has no money lacks all wisdom! If only my purse were full I could have coped with that dragon easily." Now, a merchant happened to be passing by just then, and he heard Ivan utter these words. "He's right at that!" said he. "Now, why don't I help him!" And turning to Ivan, he asked him how much money he needed. "Can you let me have five hundred rubles?" said Ivan. The merchant lent him the five hundred rubles, and Ivan hurried to the quay, hired some workmen and set them to building a ship. But he soon ran out of money and knew that unless he got more he would have to give up his venture. So he went to see the selfsame merchant and asked him for another five hundred rubles. "If I don't get them, all work will stop and you will have lost the money you gave me the first time," said he. The merchant gave him another five hundred rubles, but these too were soon used up, and the ship was still only half built. There was nothing for it, so Ivan went to see the merchant for the third time. "Give me another thousand rubles," said he, "for if you don't, all work will stop, and you will have lost all your money." This did not make the merchant any too happy, but it could not be helped, so he gave Ivan the thousand rubles. And Ivan had the ship built, took on a cargo of coal, and, taking along a bellows and some picks and shovels, put out to sea with a group of workingmen.

Whether a short time passed or a long nobody knows, but he reached the

island where the dragon had his lair and found him lying there fast asleep, gorged with food. Ivan heaped the coal he had brought all around the lair, and, making up a fire, set to fanning the flames with the bellows. Noxious fumes spread over the sea, and such was the heat that the dragon was cooked alive. Ivan brought out his sword and cut off all twelve of his heads, and, finding a precious stone in each, took them and sailed home. He sold the stones for a vast sum, became very, very rich, and having paid off his debt, set out for his hut. He was there soon enough, and whom should he see, standing beside his wife, but two tall and handsome youths. Not knowing that these were his own twin sons, born in his absence, he suspected his wife of having been unfaithful to him and seized his sword. But just as he was about to bring it down on her head, he recalled the words spoken by the old man "Never let your anger get the better of you", checked himself in time, and addressed the princess kindly, asking her to tell him who the two youths were. She told him that they were his own sons, and this filled him with such joy that he held a great feast, and they all made merry for many a day.

I was at that feast too, and *I had some wine that was sweet and light and a bun or two that were nice and white.*

Translated by Irina Zheleznova

Tereshechka

There once lived an old man and an old woman who had had a long life, but no children to show for it. In their youth they had more or less made both ends meet, but once they reached old age, there was no one to take care of them and they sorrowed and wept and did not know what to do. One day they took a piece of wood, wrapt it in some swaddling clothes, laid it in a cradle and began rocking it and singing a lullaby, and the piece of wood came alive and turned into a baby boy, an angel if ever there was one, whom they named Tereshechka. The boy grew fast and became more clever with each passing day. His father made him a little boat to go fishing in, and whenever he was out in it his mother would come to the river shore from time to time with some milk and cottage cheese for him, and, standing there, call: "Come, Tereshechka, my own little son, row to shore! *I have brought some milk for you to drink.*" And hearing her from afar, Tereshechka would row to shore, give her the fish he caught, eat and drink his fill and make off again to catch more fish.

Now, one day, after having fed him, his mother warned Tereshechka that Chuvilikha the Witch was on the watch for him. "Beware, my son, don't let her catch you!" said she. She went away, and by and by Chuvilikha came to the river shore and called out in her gruff voice: "Come, Tereshechka, my own little son, row to shore! I have brought some milk for you to drink." But Tereshechka knew it was not his mother calling and said: "Carry me farther away from the shore, little boat! That is not the voice of my mother but of Chuvilikha the

Witch." Chuvilikha went away with nothing to show for it, and soon after this Tereshechka's mother came to the river shore. "Come, Tereshechka, my own little son, row to shore!" called she in her sweet voice, and Tereshechka heard her and said: "Move, little boat, move faster, and carry me closer to shore! For that is my mother calling me." The boat brought him to the shore, and his mother gave him food and drink and sent him off fishing again.

Meanwhile Chuvilikha the Witch, having heard what Tereshechka had said about her voice, went to see a magician, got him to give her a voice as sweet as that of Tereshechka's mother, and came running back again to the river shore. She called to Tereshechka, and Tereshechka took her voice to be that of his mother and came rowing to shore. But as soon as he was close enough Chuvilikha reached out and grabbed him, and, thrusting him into a sack, ran home with him. Now, she lived in a house with chicken feet and as soon as she was, there she told her daughter to roast Tereshechka for their dinner and herself ran off again *to look for more food just as tasty and good*. But Tereshechka was no fool, and he got the better of Chuvilikha's daughter, and, thrusting her in the oven before she could do it to him, climbed a tall oak-tree.

Chuvilikha the Witch soon came running back. She rushed into her house, took the roast out of the oven, ate till she could eat no more, and, stepping out into the yard, began rolling over the grass and saying as she did so: "I'll lie on the grass and roll on it, for I ate of Tereshechka's flesh and had my fill of it!" And Tereshechka called from the top of the oak-tree: "Yes, lie on the grass and roll on it, for you ate of your own daughter's flesh and had your fill of it!" Chuvilikha heard him, she lifted her head and looked all around her, but, not seeing anyone, sang out again: "I'll lie on the grass and roll on it, for I ate of Tereshechka's flesh and had my fill of it!" But Tereshechka called again from the top of the tree: "Yes, lie on the grass and roll on it, you wicked witch, for you ate of your own daughter's flesh and had your fill of it!" Chuvilikha was frightened. She glanced up at the oak-tree, and, seeing Tereshechka, jumped up and rushed to see a blacksmith. "Please, blacksmith, forge me an axe!" cried she. The blacksmith forged her an axe, and saying, "Do not use the sharp end, use the blunt one!" gave it to her. Chuvilikha did as he said. She struck away at the tree with the blunt end of the axe, but, seeing that nothing came of it, bit into the tree and began trying to chew through it. The tree creaked and swayed, and Tereshechka knew himself to be in great danger. Now, just then a flock of Swan-Geese came flying near, and he called to them and begged them to help him.

> *"Please, Swan-Geese, heed my plea,*
> *To my folks carry me!*
> *At the door they will meet us,*
> *To a feast they will treat us!"* he called.

And the Swan-Geese called back: "Honk-honk! There's another flock of Swan-Geese coming after us. They are hungrier than we are and will be sure to help you."

Now, all this time Chuvilikha the Witch had been chewing away at the tree, and it was creaking and swaying harder than ever, and the chips were flying to all sides. Tereshechka was frightened, and, seeing a second flock of Swan-Geese come flying near, called to them and begged them to help him. *"Please, Swan-Geese, heed my plea, to my folks carry me! At the door they will meet us, to a feast they will treat us!"* he called. "Honk-honk!" the Swan-Geese called back. "There's a poor little gosling with half its feathers missing flying behind us, and it will be sure to help you." But there was no gosling in sight, and the tree under Tereshechka kept creaking and swaying and threatening to fall. And as for Chuvilikha, she would chew at it for a while and then look at Tereshechka and lick her lips before going back to chewing at it again.

But the poor little gosling with half its feathers missing *now came flying near without fear,* flapping its wings as it flew, and Tereshechka called to it and begged it to help him. *"Please, Swan-Goose, heed my plea, to my folks carry me!"* he called. *"At the door they will meet us, to a feast they will treat us!"* The poor little gosling took pity on Tereshechka. It helped him climb on its back, and, flapping its wings, flew off with him. And before long there they were flying up to Tereshechka's house and lighting on the grass under the window. Now, the old woman was holding a wake just then, and the house was packed with guests, who had come to eat of the pancakes she had baked in Tereshechka's memory. "Here's one for you, my dear," she was saying to one of them, "and one for you, old man, and one for me!" "Aren't you going to offer me one, Mother?" Tereshechka called. "I think I hear someone asking for a pancake. Go and see who it is, old man," the old woman said. The old man went outside, and, seeing Tereshechka, threw his arms round him. He led him into the house, and his mother embraced and kissed him and would not let go of him! And as for the poor little gosling with half its feathers missing, they gave it food and drink and took good care of it, and when all its feathers had grown back again, set it free. And from that time on it flew at the head of its flock, so mighty were its wings, and always spoke kindly of Tereshechka.

Translated by Irina Zheleznova

The Apples of Youth
and the Water of Life

A certain king grew very old and lost his sight. One day he heard that far, far away, at the ends of the earth, was a garden with apples of youth and a spring with the water of life. If an old man were to eat of the apples, he would grow young again, and if the water were rubbed on a blind man's eyes he would regain his sight. The king had three sons. So he sent his eldest son off on horseback to bring an apple and some water from the garden, for the king longed to regain his youth and sight. The son mounted his horse and set off for the distant land. On the way he saw a signpost pointing to three different paths. It said: take the first and your horse will be fed, but you will go hungry, take the second and you will die, take the third and your horse will go hungry, but you will be fed.

He thought hard and took the third path. On he rode until he saw a fine house standing on a plain. He rode up to it, unbolted the gate and galloped into the courtyard without doffing his cap or bowing his head. The mistress of the house, a widow not advanced in years, called the young man to her: "Hail, dear guest!" She led him into the house, sat him down at the table and gave him food and mead in abundance. So the young man ate and drank his fill and lay him down to sleep on the bench. Then the mistress of the house said:

"What self-respecting young fellow will spend the night on his own. Get you to the bed of my daughter, the fair Dunya."

He did so gladly.

"Snuggle up closer, my dear, and we will be warmer," Dunya said to him.

He moved towards her and fell through the bed into a place where he was made to thresh damp rye and could not escape. The king waited in vain for his eldest son to return and at last gave up hope.

Then the king sent his second son to bring him an apple and some water. He took the same path and shared the same fate as his elder brother. The king waited in vain for his second son to return and wept bitterly.

Then the youngest son begged his father to let him go to the garden. His father would not agree and said:

"It would be the end of you. Your elder brothers have perished, and you, a mere stripling, would perish in half the time."

But he beseeched his father, vowing to do better than his brothers. So after a while his father gave him his blessing and off he went. On the way to the widow's house everything happened just as it had to his elder brothers. He rode up to the house, dismounted, knocked at the gate and aske 1 if he could spend the night. The mistress of the house greeted him joyfully as before, saying:

"Hail, unexpected guest."

She sat him down at the table and served him all manner of food and drink. When he had eaten his fill and made to lie down on the bench, she said to him:

"No self-respecting young man sleeps alone. Get you to the bed of my fair Dunya."

But he said:

"No, mistress. That's not for a travelling man. He can kip down anywhere. How about heating up the bathhouse and letting me take your Dunya in there."

So the mistress heated up the bathhouse as hot as could be and sent him in with the fair Dunya. Now Dunya was as cunning as her mother. She sent him in first, then locked the door and stayed outside in the lobby. But the young man forced open the door and locked Dunya in there. He had three switches, one of iron, one of lead and one of copper. And he began to beat Dunya with them. She begged for mercy, but he said:

"Tell me, wicked Dunya, what have you done with my brothers?"

She told him that they were threshing damp rye in the cellar, so he let her go. Then he went into the house, tied some ladders together and brought up the brothers. He bade them go home, but they were ashamed to show their faces to the king, for they had been in the fair Dunya's bed and were good for nothing. So off they went, wandering through field and forest.

But the young prince continued on his way until he came to a house where a fair maid sat weaving towels. He went inside and said to her:

"May the good Lord help you, fair maid!"

To which she replied:

"Thank you kindly, young man. Are you on an errand or just passing the time of day?"

"I am on an errand, fair maid," said the young man. "I must go far, far away to the end of the earth to fetch the apples of youth and the water of life for my blind and aged father from the garden there."

Then she said to him:

"You've bitten off more than you can chew, trying to get to that garden. Still, if go you must, my other sister lives on the way there, so drop in to see her. She knows more than I and will tell you what to do."

So off he went until he reached the other sister. As with the first, he greeted her and told her who he was and whither he was bound. She bade him leave his horse with her and ride off on her two-winged steed to her elder sister who would tell him what to do: how to reach the garden and get the apples and water. Then off he rode again until he came to the elder sister. She gave him her four-winged steed and bade him:

"Take care, for in that garden lives our aunt, a terrible witch. When you ride up to the garden do not spare my horse. Drive him on and he will jump straight over the wall. But make sure he does not brush the wall, for on it there are strings of little bells. The strings will sound, the bells will ring, the witch will wake up and you will never escape her. She has a horse with six wings. Be sure to cut that horse's tendons, so she cannot chase you on it."

He did everything as she said. He jumped over the wall on his horse. The horse's tail brushed a string very lightly. The strings sounded and the little bells rang softly. The witch woke up, but could not hear the voices of the strings and bells properly, so she yawned and went back to sleep. And the valiant prince galloped away with the apple of youth and the water of life. On the way he dropped in to the sisters, changed horses and sped off home on his own. Early next morning the witch saw that someone had stolen the apple and water from the garden. She mounted her six-winged steed straightaway, rode to her first niece and asked her:

"Has anyone passed by here?"

Her niece replied:

"A valiant knight rode past, but that was long ago."

She galloped on and asked her second and third nieces, and they told her likewise. So on she rode and almost caught up the valiant prince, but he reached his land and no longer feared her. She dared not follow him there, and could only dart him an evil glance and cry in a voice hoarse with spite:

"No need to look so pleased with yourself, you thieving rogue. You've managed to escape from me, but your brothers will get you, just wait and see!"

Having cast this spell on him, she rode off home.

134

Our fine fellow was riding along, when he saw his vagabond brothers sleeping in a field. Not wishing to wake them, he left his horse to graze, lay down beside them and fell asleep. They woke up, saw their brother had returned, stealthily removed the apple of youth from his jacket and threw him into an abyss. Down he fell for three days until he landed in a dark underworld. Wherever he went people were weeping bitterly. When he asked the cause of their sorrow, they told him that their king's only daughter, the beautiful princess Polyusha, was going to be taken to the dragon tomorrow to be eaten up. In their land they had to give a maid to the seven-headed dragon once a month, that was the law! And now it was the princess's turn. So the valiant prince found out all about it, then went to the king himself and said:

"I will save your daughter from the dragon, Sire, but you must do what I ask of you afterwards."

The king was overjoyed and promised to do anything he asked and to give him his daughter's hand in marriage.

Next day they took the beautiful princess Polyusha down to the sea, to the three-walled fortress, and the prince went with her. He took an iron rod weighing five poods. The two of them were left there to wait for the dragon. While they were waiting they chatted about this and that. He told her about his adventure and that he had the water of life. Then he said to the beautiful princess Polyusha:

"Comb my hair. If I fall asleep and the dragon comes, hit me with my iron rod, otherwise you won't be able to wake me up!" And he put his head in her lap. She began to comb his hair and he fell asleep. The dragon flew up and hovered over the princess. She tried to wake the prince by shaking him, not wanting to hit him hard as he had bade her. When he did not wake, she began to weep, a tear fell upon his face and he started up, with a shout:

"Oh, you have burnt me with something!"

The dragon made a dive at them.

The prince picked up his five-pood rod and swung it round, knocking off five of the dragon's heads. With another blow he cut off the other two, then buried the heads under the wall and threw the body into the sea.

But a big burly fellow who had seen all this crept out from behind the wall, cut off the prince's head and threw him into the sea, bidding the Princess Polyusha tell her father, the king, that it was he who had saved her. If she did not say so, he would kill her. There was nothing for it. Polyusha wept bitterly, and off they went to her father. The king met them, and she told him that the big burly fellow had saved her. The king was overjoyed and ordered the wedding to take place. Guests came from far and wide, kings and princes, eating, drinking and making merry. Only the princess was sad. She hid in a corner by the barn, weeping bitter tears for her valiant prince.

Then she had the idea of asking her father to send fishermen down to the sea to fish, and she went with them. When they pulled in their net it was full of fish! She looked and said:

"No, my fish is not there!"

They pulled in another net and there was the head and body of the prince. Polyusha ran up quickly, found the flask with the water of life in his jacket, put the head on the body, sprinkled it with the water, and he came to life again. She told him how the hateful burly fellow wanted to marry her. The prince comforted her and told her to go home. He would take care of everything.

So the prince went to the king's palace where the drunken guests were dancing and singing. He said he could play all sorts of songs. They were pleased and bade him play. First he played a merry ditty. They liked it so much, that they praised him to the skies. Then he played such a sad song that they began to cry. Then the prince asked the king who had rescued his daughter. The king said it was the burly fellow.

"In that case let's go to the fortress with all the guests, Sire. If he can pull out the dragon's heads, I will believe he rescued Princess Polyusha."

So they all went down to the fortress. The burly fellow pulled and pulled, but he could not pull out a single head. He hadn't the strength. The prince pulled them out in a twinkling. Then the princess told the truth about who had rescued her. When they all realised that it was the prince who had rescued the king's daughter, they tied the burly fellow to a horse's tail and dragged him over hill and dale.

The king wanted the prince to marry his daughter, but the prince said:

"No, Sire, I want nothing but to go up from the underworld. I have not yet finished my father's errand. He is waiting for me to bring the water of life to cure his blindness."

The king did not know how to send the prince up from the underworld. The princess would not be parted from her rescuer and wanted to go up with him. She told her father that they had a big bird who could carry them up, provided it had enough food for the journey.

So Polyusha bade them kill an ox for the bird. Then they bade the king farewell, climbed onto the bird's back and flew up to the sunlight. When they gave the bird a lot to eat, it carried them up more quickly. Soon it had gobbled up the whole ox. Now they were afraid it would carry them down again. There was nothing for it, so Polyusha cut off a piece of her thigh and gave it to the bird. Then the bird flew up into the sunlight and said:

"You have fed me well all the way, but that last morsel was the sweetest I have ever tasted."

Polyusha showed her where the morsel was from and the bird gasped with amazement and coughed up the slice. Then the prince placed it back, sprinkled it with the water of life and the princess's thigh was whole again.

At last they arrived at the palace. The king met them, overwhelmed with joy. The prince saw that his father had regained his youth from the apple but was still blind. So he straightaway rubbed his eyes with the water of life, and the king began to see again. He kissed the valiant prince and the beautiful princess from the dark underworld. Then the prince told him how his brothers had taken away the apple and cast him into the underworld. The brothers were so afraid that they jumped into the river. But the valiant prince married Polyusha and they had a fine wedding feast. I there did dine and drank mead wine with cabbage aplenty, but now my mouth's empty!

Translated by K. M. Cook-Horujy

The Petrified Kingdom

In a certain kingdom, in a certain realm there was once a soldier who served the king honestly many a year. A neat man he was and went by the rules, and you never saw him at drills and exercises but with boots polished and buttons shined. But the officers frowned on him, and many were the times they had him thrashed or birched.

It was a hard life, and though he was now in his last year of service, the soldier made up his mind to run away. He hung his knapsack on his back and his rifle over his shoulder, and he bade his comrades goodbye. "Where are you off to? Does the commander want you?" they asked him. "Never you mind, brothers, just help me pull these straps tighter and think well of me once I'm gone," the soldier said. And away he went where the road led.

Whether a short or a long time passed nobody knows, but there came a day when he made his way across the border and found himself in a foreign land. He saw a sentry and asked him if there was a place there where he could rest. The sentry passed this on to a corporal, the corporal to an officer, the officer to a general, and the general to the king, who ordered the soldier to be ushered into the palace. The soldier was led in, and he stood before the king like one rooted to the spot, as the rules demanded, his rifle held straight in front of him. "Tell me where you come from and where you are going, soldier, and mind, don't

keep anything back," said the king. "I'll tell you all, Your Majesty, only do be merciful and don't have me punished," the soldier said. He told the king all about everything and begged him to take him into his service. "Would you like to be a watchman?" the king asked. "Someone has been coming to my garden and felling my trees, and if you do your best and keep them from doing it I'll pay you well." And the soldier agreed to this and began watching over the garden.

He watched over it for a year and for two years and all went well, but just as the third year was coming to an end, he found that a half of all the trees had been felled. "Dear me, what a terrible thing to have happened!" said he to himself. "When the king finds out about this, he will have me hanged!" He took his rifle in his hands, leant against a tree and stood there, thinking. All of a sudden there came a loud crash, and he saw a huge, fearful-looking bird bringing down a tree. He put a bullet through its wing, and the bird, wounded, started away, losing three of its feathers as it did so. He ran after it, but the bird proved to be a fast runner, and before he knew it it got to a hole in the ground and was lost to sight.

Now the soldier being no coward, he leapt after it, but the hole was very deep, and he hurt himself badly as he hit the ground and fainted dead away, and it was not till a day and a night had passed that he came to. He rose and looked round him, and, hard as it was to believe, it was as light there as out on top. "There must be people living here somewhere," thought he. He set out on his way, he walked and he walked, and he came to a big city with a sentry-house in front of the gate and a sentry beside it. The soldier spoke to him, but the sentry did not answer; he touched his hand, and it was ice-cold. He came into the sentry-house, and there were men there, some sitting, some standing, but all as if made of stone. He walked through the gate and roamed the streets, but there was not a living soul in sight. He came to a palace with pictured walls and marched inside, but though the chambers were richly decorated and there was food and drink on the tables, all was silence and emptiness.

The soldier ate and drank and had just sat down for a rest when he heard, coming from the street, a sound as of a carriage driving up and drawing to a stop. He grabbed his rifle, ran to the door and stood there at attention, and in came a most beautiful princess escorted by her women and maids. The soldier's hand flew up in a salute, and the princess smiled and nodded her head. "Greetings, soldier!" said she. "Tell me what brought you here." The soldier told her about how he had become the king's watchman and about the bird that felled the trees in the king's garden. "I shot it through the wing, and when it rushed away I followed it and found myself here," said he. "That bird is my own sister," the princess said, "but she is an evil sorceress who turned all my people to stone. Now listen to me. Here is a book for you, and no matter what terrible things you seem to see happening about you, you must stand here and read it from dusk to cockcrow. If you let anyone pull it out of your grasp you will be done for, but if three nights pass and you hold out, then you and I will be married." "I'll do as you say!" said the soldier, and the moment evening came he picked up the book.

All of a sudden there came a great stamping of boots and a clangour of arms, and a whole army stormed into the palace. The soldier was surrounded by his former officers, who began cursing him and threatening to have him put to death for having run away. But though they loaded their rifles and pointed them at him, the soldier never looked at them and went on reading. Then the cocks crowed, everything vanished, and it was as if it had never been. The following night was even more fearful, and the third night so terrifying that the soldier did not think he could bear it, for the palace was overrun by hangmen and torturers who came there with saws, hammers and axes and threatened to crush his bones, stretch him on a rack and burn him at the stake. They tried again and again to snatch the book from him, but the soldier held on to it for dear life and would not let go. Then the cocks crowed, everything vanished, and it was as if it had never been. The same moment the whole of the kingdom and all of the people in it came to life, and into the palace stepped the beautiful princess followed by her nobles and generals. They thanked the soldier again and again and made him king, and he and the princess were married and lived happily ever after.

Translated by Irina Zheleznova

The Wood Goblin

There was once a priest's daughter who without asking her parents' permission went for a walk in the forest one day and never came back. And when three years had passed, there was still not a sign or a sight of her. Now, in the village she had lived in there was a brave young hunter who would let not a day pass without going out hunting with his dog. One day they were out together in the thickest part of the forest when the dog bristled and began to bark. The hunter looked up, and there on the path before him he saw a man sitting on a log mending a bast shoe. The strips of bast were loose, and he would pull up one of them and then shake his finger at the moon and say: "Shine bright, moon!" over and over again. The hunter was filled with wonder. Not only was the man behaving strangely but, too, though he looked young and fit, his hair was snow-white. And the thought had no sooner passed through his head than the man seemed to guess what it was, for he said: "You need not be amazed, my lad; I am, you see, the devil's granddad!" It was then that the hunter knew that the man was no ordinary man but a wood goblin. He pointed his gun at him and fired, and the bullet hit the goblin in the belly. The goblin let out a moan and nearly fell over, but he managed to regain his feet and drag himself into the thicket. The dog ran after him, and the hunter went after the dog.

On and on he walked and he came to a hill with a cleft in it and a hut half

hidden in the cleft. He stepped into the hut, and there was the goblin stretched out on a bench with a girl sitting beside him. The goblin was dead, and the girl was weeping bitterly and saying over and over again, "What am I to do! Who is going to take care of me now!" "Good morrow, fair maid!" said the hunter. "Where do you come from and who are your mother and father?" "Ah, brave youth, that is something I do not know," said the girl. "It's as if I never had a mother or a father or been out of this forest!" "Well, then, come, and I'll take you to my village," said the hunter. And taking the girl by the hand, he began leading her out of the forest, leaving a mark on every tree they passed. Now, the girl had been carried off by the goblin and had stayed with him for three whole years, so her clothes were worn to tatters. But though she was practically stark naked, she knew no shame.

They came to the village, and the hunter began asking everyone if they had not lost a daughter or a niece of theirs some years back. And the priest looked at the girl, and, knowing her to be his child, cried: "That is my daughter!" And his wife came running and burst out with: "Oh, my dear child, where have you been all this time? I never thought to see you again!" But the girl only looked at her wide-eyed ans could not make out what she meant. By and by, however, she came to a little and recalled the past, and her parents had her marry the hunter and gave him many fine presents to reward him for having saved her. But though they wandered round the forest for a long time looking for the hut she had lived in with the goblin, they never found it.

Translated by Irina Zheleznova

Dead Men's Tales

One night a peasant was riding along with some pots. His horse was tired and stopped by a graveyard.

The peasant unharnessed the horse and let it graze, while he lay down on a grave. For some reason he just could not get to sleep. He lay there for a while, until suddenly the grave beneath him began to open. He felt it and jumped up.

The grave opened wide and out climbed a dead man in a white shroud with a coffin lid, ran to the church, stood the coffin lid in the doorway and hurried off to the village.

The peasant was a brave man. He took the coffin lid and waited by his cart to see what would happen.

A little later back came the dead man. He looked for the coffin lid, but it was not there. So he traced his way back to the cart along the peasant's footprints, reached him and said:

"Give me back my lid, or I'll tear you to pieces."

"See this axe?" the peasant replied. "I'll hack you to bits with it."

"Give me the lid, be a good fellow," the dead man begged him.

"I'll give it back, if you tell me where you've been and what you've done."

"I've been down to the village and I killed two young lads."

"Well, you just tell me how to bring them to life again."

The dead man was forced to tell him.

"Cut the left side off my shroud and take it with you. When you get to the house where the lads were killed, put some burning coals in a pot with the piece of shroud and lock the door. The smoke will bring them to life again."

The peasant cut the left side off the shroud and gave back the coffin lid.

The dead man walked up to the grave, the grave opened, but just as he was about to climb in the cocks crowed, and he could not cover himself up properly. One end of the lid remained outside.

The peasant saw all this and took note of it. Day began to break. He harnessed his horse and set off for the village.

In one house he heard weeping and moaning. He went in and there lay the two dead lads.

"Don't weep. I can bring them back to life again."

"Then do so, dear friend, and you shall have half of all we possess," said their family.

The peasant did everything the dead man had told him, and the lads came to life again.

Their relatives were delighted, but they seized the peasant and tied him up.

"You are a sorcerer! We'll hand you over to the authorities. If you could bring them to life, you must have killed them too!"

"Come now, fellow Christians! Fear the Lord!" cried the peasant, and told them what had happened that night.

So they called all the villagers together and went off to the graveyard, found the grave which had opened and hammered an aspen stake right through the heart of the dead man so he would not rise up anymore and kill people. And then they rewarded the peasant handsomely and sent him home with due honour.

A certain soldier was given leave to go home. He walked for many a long mile until he was close to his native village.

Not far from the village lived a miller in his mill. In the old days he and the soldier had been great friends. Why not drop in to see him now? The soldier dropped in and was greeted warmly by the miller, who brought out some wine at once. They began to drink and talk about how life was treating them. It was, getting on for evening. While the soldier sat drinking with the miller darkness fell. The soldier was about to leave for the village, when the miller said:

"Spend the night here, friend. It's late and you'd be sure to get into trouble."

"Why is that?"

"The good Lord has punished us! A terrible sorcerer died here, and at night he rises from the grave and wanders round the village doing things that would make the bravest men's hair stand on end! I fear he might harm you."

"Never fear. A soldier belongs to the state, and state property does not sink in water or burn in fire. I am in a hurry to see my family."

So off he went. The path ran past the graveyard. On one grave he saw a light shining.

"What's that? Let's take a look."

He crept up and there, by the light, sat the sorcerer stitching his boots.

"Hail, brother!" the soldier called to him.

The sorcerer looked up and asked:

"Why have you come here?"

"I just wanted to see what you were doing."

The sorcerer put aside his work and asked the soldier to come to a wedding with him.

"Let's go and make merry, brother. There's a wedding in the village tonight."

"Right, come on."

They went to the wedding and were given plenty to eat and drink. The sorcerer drank like a fish, until he ran amuck and chased all the guests and relations out of the house, sent the bride and groom to sleep, took out two bottles and an awl, pierced the arms of the bride and groom with the awl and filled the bottles with their blood. Then he said to the soldier:

"Now let's be on our way."

So off they went. On the way the soldier asked:

"Why did you fill those bottles with their blood?"

"So that the bride and groom would die. Tomorrow nobody will be able to waken them. Only I know how to bring them to life."

"And how is that?"

"You must cut the heels of the bride and groom and pour their blood into the wounds, the right blood for the right person. In my right pocket is the groom's blood and in my left the bride's."

The soldier listened without uttering a word. And the sorcerer kept boasting:

"I do just as I like."

"It looks as if no one can get the better of you."

"Can't they just? If they pile up a hundred cartloads of aspen wood into a bonfire and burn me on it, that will be the end of me. Only they must do it properly. For all sorts of snakes, worms and other vermin will crawl out of my belly and out will fly jackdaws, magpies and ravens. You must catch them and throw them into the fire. If a single worm escapes, it will all be in vain! I shall slip away in that worm."

148

The soldier listened and took note of what the sorcerer said. They talked on and on until they reached the grave.

"Now I must tear you to pieces, brother," said the sorcerer. "Or you will tell all."

"Have some sense! How can you tear me to pieces? I serve God and the Tsar."

The sorcerer gnashed his teeth, howled and leapt at the soldier. But the soldier drew his sabre and parried the blows. On and on they fought until the soldier was almost at the end of his tether. "I'm finished," he thought, "and all for nothing."

Suddenly the cocks crowed and the sorcerer collapsed lifeless. The soldier took the bottles of blood out of the sorcerer's pockets and went home to his family.

When he arrived and greeted them, his relatives asked him:

"Did you see anything wrong, soldier?"

"No, I didn't."

"There's great misfortune in the village. A sorcerer has started rampaging round our homes."

They talked for a while, then went to bed. In the morning the soldier woke up and asked:

"Isn't there a wedding going on here?"

"There was a wedding at the rich man's house," his relatives replied. "But the bride and groom died last night, of what nobody knows."

"And where does that rich man live?"

They told him where the house was. Without a word he went there and found the whole family in tears.

"Why are you weeping?"

They told him what had happened.

"What will you give me, if I bring the young couple to life again?"

"Half of all we possess."

The soldier did as the sorcerer had told him and brought the young people to life. Instead of tears, there was laughter and rejoicing.

The soldier was wined, dined and rewarded handsomely. Then he went left march to the village elder and told him to summon the peasants together and prepare a hundred cartloads of aspen logs.

They carried the firewood to the graveyard, piled it up, dragged the sorcerer out of his grave, put him on the fire and set light to him. All round the fire stood the people with brooms, spades and pokers. The flames leapt up and the sorcerer began to burn. His belly burst. Out crawled snakes, worms and all manner of vermin, and out flew ravens, magpies and jackdaws. The men struck them and threw them into the fire. Not one worm managed to escape. And so the sorcerer was burnt! The soldier collected his ashes at once and cast them to the winds.

Since then all has been peaceful in the village. All the villagers thanked the soldier. He spent his leave in his native parts, had a rollicking time and returned to the Tsar's service with money in his pockets. In due course he retired from the army and began to live and prosper with not a care in the world.

A certain soldier asked for leave to visit his native village and see his family. He set off and walked for three days until he reached a dense forest. Where was he to spend the night? In a glade he saw two houses, went into the first and found an old woman there.

"Good-day, Granny."

"Good-day to you, soldier boy."

"Can I spend the night here?"

"Aye, but you won't find it any too comfortable."

"Why? Isn't there much room? Don't you worry, Granny. A soldier doesn't need a lot of space. I'll curl up in a corner. Anywhere but outside."

"No, it's not that, lad. There's trouble aplenty round here..."

"What trouble?"

"I'll tell you what. An old man died in the house next door not so long ago—a terrible sorcerer, he was. And now each night he comes rampaging round the houses and eating people."

"Don't worry, Granny."

The soldier took off his coat, had supper and climbed onto the stove bench, placing his cutlass beside him. At the stroke of midnight all the bolts slid back and the doors opened wide. Into the house came the dead man in a white shroud and seized hold of the old woman.

"Why have you come here, accursed one?" the soldier shouted at him.

The sorcerer let go of the old woman, leapt onto the stove bench and began grappling with the soldier. The soldier struck him again and again with his cutlass, cutting off all his fingers, but could not get the better of him. Locked together hard, they both fell off the bench onto the floor, the sorcerer landing under the soldier. The soldier grabbed him by the beard and laboured him with his cutlass until the cocks crowed. At that moment the sorcerer went rigid, like a log, lying there without moving.

The soldier dragged him into the yard and threw him head first down the well. He saw the fine pair of new hobnailed boots on the sorcerer's feet. "'Tis a pity to waste them," he thought. "Let's take them off." So he took off the dead man's boots and went back into the house.

"Oh, my goodness, soldier," said the old woman. "Why did you take off his boots?"

"Why leave them on him? Just look what a fine pair. Anyone would give at, least a silver rouble for them, and I'm forever on the march. They're just the job for me."

The next day the soldier took his leave of the old woman and went on his way. But wherever he spent the night at the stroke of midnight the sorcerer would appear under the window and demand his boots.

"I will give you no peace," he threatened. "I will follow you everywhere, on leave and on service."

The soldier could stand it no longer.

"What is it you want, accursed one?"

"Give me back my boots!"

The soldier threw them out of the window.

"Now leave me alone, you devil."

The sorcerer grabbed the boots, whistled and vanished into thin air.

Translated by K. M. Cook-Horujy

Witches' Tales

Late one evening a Cossack arrived in a village, stopped at the first house he came to and asked the owner if he could stay the night there.

"Aye, if you're not afraid of death."

"What is he talking about!" thought the Cossack. He left his horse in the barn, gave it some fodder and went into the house.

There he found men, women and little children weeping bitterly and praying to the good Lord. After the prayers they put on clean shirts and shifts.

"Why are you crying?" asked the Cossack.

"Death stalks our village at night," said the master of the house, "and if she looks into a window all the people in that house will be carried to the graveyard in coffins the next morning. It's our turn tonight."

"Don't be afraid, friend."

The man and his wife went to bed, but the Cossack kept on the alert.

At the stroke of midnight the window flew open and a witch appeared, dressed all in white. She took an aspergillum, thrust an arm into the room and was about to start sprinkling when the Cossack swung his sabre and cut off her arm at the shoulder. The witch gasped, screamed, yelped like a dog and ran away. And the Cossack picked up the severed arm, hid it under his greatcoat, washed away the blood and went to sleep.

The next morning the man and his wife woke up to find everyone hale and hearty and were overjoyed.

"Shall I show you death?" said the Cossack. "Gather up all your able-bodied men and come to look for her in the village."

When all the able-bodied men were gathered, they set off round the houses. They found nothing until at last they reached the sexton's house.

"Is all your family here?" asked the Cossack.

"No, friend! One of our daughters is ill. She's lying on the stove bench."

The Cossack looked at her and saw that one of her arms was cut off. He straightway told them what had happened and showed them the arm.

The villagers rewarded the Cossack with money and had the witch drowned.

In a certain land there was once a king whose daughter was a sorceress. In the king's court was a priest. The priest had a son of ten who went to an old woman each day to learn to read and write. One day he was coming home late from his lesson. Walking past the palace, he happened to glance up at a small window. By it sat the princess. She took off her head, washed it with soap and water, combed and plaited the hair, then put her head on again. The boy could scarce believe his eyes. "Ee, she's a sly one! Must be a witch!" He went home and told everyone he had seen the princess without her head.

Suddenly the king's daughter fell ill. She summoned her father and told him:

"If I die, make the priest's son read the Psalter over me three nights running."

And die she did. They put her in a coffin and carried her into the church.

Then the king called the priest to him.

"Do you have a son?"

"Aye, Your Majesty."

"Then let him read the Psalter over my daughter three nights running."

The priest went home and told his son to get ready.

In the morning the priest's son went to his lesson and sat sadly over his book.

"Why are you so sad?" asked the old woman.

"How can I help being sad, if my end is nigh."

"What's the matter? Talk sense."

"I have to read the Psalter over the princess, Granny, but she is a sorceress."

"I knew that before you. Never fear, just take this knife and when you go into the church draw a circle around yourself with it and read the Psalter without looking round. Keep on reading whatever happens, no matter what terrible things you imagine. If you look round, it will be the end of you."

That evening the boy went to the church, drew a circle round himself with the knife and began to read the Psalter. At the stroke of midnight, the lid rose from the coffin, the princess stood up and ran out, crying:

"Now I'll teach you to spy on me under my window and tell everybody."

She rushed at the priest's son, but could not cross into the circle. So then she got up to all sorts of tricks, but he went on reading and never once looked

154

round. At daybreak the princess ran back to her coffin and flopped down into it.

The next night the same thing happened. The priest's son was not afraid of anything and read on without stopping until daybreak. In the morning he went to the old woman.

"Well, did you see some terrible things?" she asued.

"I did, Granny."

"Today it will be even more terrible! Take this hammer and four nails, knock them into the four corners of the coffin, and when you start reading the Psalter place the hammer in front of you."

That evening the priest's son went into the church and did as the old woman had told him. At the stroke of midnight the coffin lid fell onto the floor. The princess rose up and began to fly about in all directions, threatening the priest's son. She conjured up things each more terrible than the last. At one moment the priest's son thought the church was on fire, for the walls were a sheet of flame. But he went on reading and did not look round. At the crack of dawn the princess ran into her coffin, the flames disappeared and the terrible vision vanished.

That morning the king came to the church and saw that the coffin was open and the princess was lying face down.

"What's the matter?" he asked the boy.

The boy told him all that had happened. Then the king ordered them to drive an aspen stake into his daughter's heart and bury her in the ground, and rewarded the priest's son with money and land.

Translated by K. M. Cook-Horujy

The Daring Workman

There was once a miller who had a workman. One day the miller told the workman to go to the mill and grind some wheat, and not knowing how to go about it, the workman poured the wheat on to the millstone. The millstone began turning round and round, the wheat was scattered over the floor, and when the miller came to the mill and saw what had happened, he drove the workman out. The workman set out for his village but got lost on the way, and, coming to some tall bushes, went behind them and lay down for a sleep. By and by a wolf came running up, and, seeing the workman lying there, began sniffing at him. But the workman woke up, and, seizing the wolf by the tail, killed and then skinned it.

After this he walked on and after a time came to a knoll, on top of which stood an empty mill. He had just settled down for the night near the mill when three men, three robbers, came riding up to it. Seeing them, the workman rushed into the mill and dived into the tun, and he had just done so when the robbers stepped inside. They made up a fire and began dividing their money. "I'm going to put my money in the cellar," said the first robber; "I'm going to find a place for mine under the wheel," said the second robber; "And I'm going to hide mine in the tun," said the third robber. And the workman lay there trembling, and, afraid that the robbers might kill him, told himself that he must find a way of frightening them off. So he shouted very loudly: *"Quick, Dennis friend, and Khvoka, you too, give them a beating that's what we'll do! Seize them, lads, hold them, punch them, all three. Teach them a lesson we will, you shall see!"*

The robbers were scared half out of their wits. They threw down their money and took to their heels.

And the workman climbed out of the tun, picked up the money and went home. He told his mother and father about all that had happened to him and showed them the money. "See what I have earned at the mill!" said he. "And now let's go to market, Father. We'll buy ourselves a gun and make our living hunting." They went to market and bought themselves a gun, and it was when they were on their way home that the workman said to his father: "Keep your eyes open, Father, for it might just happen that we will come across a hare, a fox or a marten." But they felt drowsy, both of them, and as they rode along, began to nod and were soon fast asleep. All of a sudden, as if out of nowhere, two wolves appeared, killed their horse and ate it up. The old man woke with a start and waved his whip, thinking to goad on the horse, but he hit one of the wolves instead. The wolf backed away, found himself with the yoke round his neck and ran for his life, bearing the wagon after him. And as for the other wolf, he tried to bite the workman, but the workman struck him with his whip, and, there being a knot in it, it got stuck in a hole between the wolf's teeth where one of them was missing! So now there was the first wolf bearing the wagon along, and the second wolf, being dragged behind it. They were soon home, and, seeing them, the watchdog jumped out of the kennel and began to bark. And this so frightened the wolves that one of them turned round sharply and overturned the wagon, sending the workman and his father rolling out on to the ground and shaking off the yoke at the same time. The second wolf too was set free, for the workman let the whip out of his hands, the two wolves ran away, and the workman and his father were left with nothing to show for it! *But they led a rich life, as I have been told, and their house with its yard was a joy to behold! It was made of three poles and three switches in all, had the sky for a roof and the plain for a wall.*

Translated by Irina Zheleznova

Hocus-Pocus

In a certain kingdom, in a certain realm, there lived a sailor. He served the king loyally, treated his fellow-men honestly and so was known to the authorities. One day he asked for leave to go ashore. He put on his best uniform and went to a tavern. There he sat down at a table and ordered wine and food. Soon he had eaten and drunk a good ten roubles worth, but he kept on ordering more.

"Now then, sailor boy," said the waiter. "You're putting a lot away, but have you got the wherewithal to pay for it?"

"So you don't think I can afford all this, eh? Why, I've got money to burn, lad."

He took a gold coin out of his pocket and threw it on the table, saying:

"There, take that."

The waiter picked up the gold coin, totted up the bill and brought the sailor the change. But the sailor said:

"Don't bother about the change, lad! Buy yourself some vodka with it."

The next day the sailor asked for leave again, went into the same tavern and spent another gold coin. On the third day the same thing happened, and he began to go there almost every day and pay in gold coins, never taking the change, but leaving it for the waiter. The tavern-keeper noticed this and became suspicious. "What can it mean? He's just an ordinary sailor, yet he comes here throwing money around. He's spent a whole box of gold coins. I know how much sailors are paid—a mere pittance! He's most likely stolen it from somew-

here. I must tell the authorities, or I'll get into trouble myself, if I don't look out, and end up in Siberia."

So the tavern keeper told the officer and the officer reported it to the general himself. The general summoned the sailor.

"You just own up," he said. "Where did you get all that gold from?"

"Why, you can find heaps of those gold coins in any rubbish pit."

"Why are you lying?"

"I'm not lying, Your Excellency. It's the tavern-keeper who's lying. Ask him to show you the gold he got from me."

They brought out the box, opened it and it was full of bones.

"Now then, my fellow. You paid in gold, but it has turned into bones. How did you manage to do that?"

"Alas, Your Excellency! Death is nigh..."

They looked round and saw water pouring in through the doors and windows. It rose higher and higher until it was up to their chins.

"Oh, my goodness! What can we do? How can we get out?" the general asked in alarm.

To which the sailor replied:

"If you don't want to drown, Your Excellency, climb up the chimney after me."

So they climbed up the chimney onto the roof and looked round them. The whole town was flooded! The water was so high that in some parts the houses were no longer to be seen, and it was rising all the time.

"Well, brother," said the general. "It looks as though you and I have had it too."

"I don't know. We'll see about that."

"My death is nigh," thought the general, standing in despair and praying to the good Lord.

Suddenly out of thin air a small boat floated up, got caught on the roof and stopped there.

"Get in quickly, Your Excellency," said the sailor, "and let's sail away. Perhaps we'll survive, if the water goes down soon."

So they both got into the boat and the wind carried them off. On the third day the water began to go down, so quickly they couldn't believe their eyes. It was soon dry all around. They got out of the boat and asked the good folk where the waves had brought them and how far they were from home. It turned out that they were in the thrice-ten kingdom beyond thrice-nine land. The folk there were strange and foreign. How could they get home again? They hadn't a bean, anything to help them on their way. The sailor said:

"We must get a job and earn some money. Otherwise we'll never get home."

"It's all very well for you, brother. You're used to working, but what about me? I'm a general, as you know, and I don't know how to work."

"Don't worry, I'll find the sort of work that anyone can do."

So they went to a village and offered to tend the cattle. The villagers agreed and took them on for the whole summer. The sailor was put in charge with the general to help him. So they tended the cattle until autumn, then collected their pay and set about dividing it up.

The sailor divided it equally, the same for himself as for the general. When the general saw that the sailor was getting the same as him he took offence and said:

"How can you think you are equal to me? After all, I'm a general and you're just a common sailor."

"Think yourself lucky. I should really divide the money into three, two parts for myself and one part for you. After all I was the real shepherd and you just helped me."

The general grew angry and began to curse the sailor. But the sailor stood firm. In the end he waved his hand and gave the general a dig in the ribs.

"Wake up, Your Excellency!"

The general woke up and looked around him. He was in his room, as if he had never left it, and everything was as it had always been. Having no wish to question the sailor further, he let him go, and the tavern-keeper did not get a penny.

Translated by K. M. Cook-Horujy

The Biter Bit

A certain soldier arrived at a village and asked a peasant to put him up for the night.

"I would gladly, friend," the man replied. "But we're having a wedding here and there's nowhere for you to sleep."

"Don't worry. A soldier can sleep anywhere."

The soldier saw that the peasant's horse was harnessed to the sledge and asked:

"Where are you going, friend?"

"Well, there's a custom in these parts. If you are holding a wedding you must first visit the sorcerer and take him a present! The poorest man can't get away with less than twenty roubles, and if you're rich it costs you a good fifty. If you don't give him anything, he'll ruin the wedding for you."

"Listen, friend. Don't give him anything, it'll be alright."

He was so persuasive that the man followed his advice and did not take the sorcerer any presents.

So the wedding procession set off on sledges for the church. As they were riding along, a bull came charging towards them, roaring loudly and tossing its horns. Everyone was terrified, only the soldier did not move a hair. Suddenly out from under him sprang a dog. It leapt at the bull, seized it by the throat and the bull crashed to the ground.

They drove on and suddenly saw a huge bear coming towards them.

"Don't be afraid," cried the soldier. "I won't let it harm you."

Again out from under him sprang a dog which leapt at the bear and seized it by the throat. The bear gave a great roar and dropped dead.

That danger past, they drove on once more. Then a hare came running towards the procession and leapt across the road almost under the very feet of the first team of horses. The horses came to a halt, snorting, and would not budge.

"That's enough of your tricks, hare," the soldier cried. "We'll deal with you later." And immediately the whole procession set off again.

They reached the church safely, where the two were duly wed, and then set off back to the village.

As they were approaching the house, a black raven sitting on the gate began to caw loudly. The horses stopped again and would not budge.

"That's enough of your tricks, raven," the soldier cried. "We'll deal with you later."

The raven flew away and the horses trotted into the yard.

So the bridal pair were seated and the guests and relations took their places, all as it should be, and they ate, drank and made merry. But the sorcerer was furious because they hadn't given him any presents and all his attempts to ruin the wedding had been in vain.

So he arrived at the house in person. He did not take off his hat, pray to the icons or bow to the assembled company, only said to the soldier:

"I'm angry with you."

"What for? I haven't borrowed from you, and you don't owe me anything. Let's better drink and make merry."

"Very well."

The sorcerer picked up a flagon of beer, poured a glass and took it to the soldier.

"Drink up, soldier boy."

The soldier drank it, and all his teeth fell into the glass.

"Oh, brother," said the soldier. "How can I do without my teeth? What will I munch rusks with?"

He took his teeth, put them in his mouth, and they were just as they had always been.

"Now I'll get you a glass of beer, and you must drink it."

The sorcerer drank it and his eyes popped out. The soldier caught them and threw them away.

So the sorcerer went blind, repented his tricks and left good folk in peace. And from that day on the villagers remembered the soldier in their prayers.

Translated by K. M. Cook-Horujy

The Exchange

One day, a peasant, who was cleaning a cowhouse of dung, found an oat grain. He came into his house where his wife had the stove going and said:

"Come, wife, step lively! Rake out the coals, put this grain into the oven, and when it's baked, take it out, pound it and grind it, make a jelly out of it and pour the jelly into a plate. I'll take the plate of jelly to the tsar, and perhaps he'll give me something in reward for it."

The wife did as he asked, and he brought the plate of jelly to the tsar and got a golden bun from him in reward.

As he was on his way home with the bun he happened to be crossing a field where a herd of horses was being pastured.

"Have you been far away, peasant?" he herdsman asked him.

"*No, not far. I saw the tsar,* and I gave him a plate of jelly."

"And what did the tsar give you in reward?"

"A golden bun."

"Give me the bun, and I'll give you a horse in return for it."

The peasant gave the herdsman the golden bun, got a horse from him in return for it, mounted it and rode away.

By and by he saw a herd of cows being pastured.

"Have you been far away, peasant?" the herdsman asked him.

"No, not far. I saw the tsar, and I gave him a plate of jelly."

"What did the tsar give you in reward?"

"A golden bun."

"Where is it?"

"I exchanged it for this horse."

"Give me the horse, and I'll give you a cow in return for it."

The peasant gave the herdsman his horse, got a cow in return for it and, leading the cow by the horns, went away. By and by he came to a place where a flock of sheep was grazing.

"Have you been far away, peasant?" the shepherd asked him.

"No, not far. I saw the tsar, and I gave him a plate of jelly."

"What did the tsar give you in reward?"

"A golden bun."

"Where is it?"

"I exchanged it for a horse."

"Where is the horse?"

"I exchanged it for a cow."

"Well, then, give me the cow, and I'll give you a sheep in return for it."

The peasant gave the shepherd the cow, got a sheep from him in return for it, and, driving the sheep ahead of him, walked on.

By and by he came to a place where a man was tending some pigs.

"Have you been far away, peasant?" the man asked.

"No, not far. I saw the tsar, and I gave him a plate of jelly."

"What did the tsar give you in reward?"

"A golden bun."

"Where is it?"

"I exchanged it for a horse."

"Where is the horse?"

"I exchanged it for a cow."

"Where is the cow?"

"I exchanged it for a sheep."

"Well, then, give me the sheep, and I'll give you a pig in return for it."

The peasant gave the man the sheep, got a pig in return for it and went on. By and by he saw a man tending a flock of geese.

"Have you been far away, peasant?" the man asked.

"No, not far. I saw the tsar, and I gave him a plate of jelly."

"What did the tsar give you in reward?"

"A golden bun."

"Where is it?"

"I exchanged it for a horse."

"Where is the horse?"

"I exchanged it for a cow."

"Where is the cow?"

"I exchanged it for a sheep."

"Where is the sheep?"

"I exchanged it for a pig."

"Well, then, give me the pig, and I'll give you a goose in return for it."

The peasant gave the pig to the man, got a goose in return for it and went on.

By and by he met a man who was tending some ducks.

"Have you been far away, peasant?" the man asked.

"*No, not far. I saw the tsar,* and I gave him a plate of jelly."

"What did the tsar give you in reward?"

"A golden bun."

"Where is it?"

"I exchanged it for a horse."

"Where is the horse?"

"I exchanged it for a cow."

"Where is the cow?"

"I exchanged it for a sheep."

"Where is the sheep?"

"I exchanged it for a pig."

"Where is the pig?"

"I exchanged it for a goose."

"Well, then, give me the goose, and I'll give you a duck in return for it."

The peasant gave the man the goose, got a duck in return for it and went on. By and by he saw some boys playing a game of bandy.

"Have you been far away, peasant?" the boys asked him.

"*No, not far. I saw the tsar,* and I gave him a plate of jelly."

"What did the tsar give you in reward?"

"A golden bun."

"Where is it?"

"I exchanged it for a horse."

"Where is the horse?"

"I exchanged it for a cow."

"Where is the cow?"

"I exchanged it for a sheep."

"Where is the sheep?"

"I exchanged it for a pig."

"Where is the pig?"

"I exchanged it for a goose."

"Where is the goose?"

"I exchanged it for a duck."

"Well, then, give us the duck, and we'll give you a bandy in return for it."

The peasant gave the duck to the boys, got a bandy in return for it and went on. He came to his house, left the bandy by the gate and went inside. His wife asked him how he had fared, and he told her all about everything.

"Where is the bandy?" his wife asked.

"By the gate where I left it."

The wife brought the bandy into the house and fell on her husband, hitting him over the back and head with it.

"Take that, you old fool!" she cried. "You might at least have brought home the duck!"

Translated by Irina Zheleznova

Foma Berennikov

In a certain kingdom, in a certain realm there once lived a peasant by the name of Foma Berennikov who was so hardy and strong that if a sparrow were to fly past him and brush him with its wing, his knees would buckle under him and he would fall to the ground. It was a sad life he led, for everyone treated him badly, and one day he told himself that he would drown himself and end it all! He came up to a swamp, and when the frogs saw him they all jumped down into the water. "No, I'm not going to drown myself after all," said Foma, "for there are some who are afraid of me!" He came back home and made ready to go to the field to plough. Now, his horse was a poor, overworked nag, its neck rubbed so raw by its collar that the flies and gad-flies clung to it in swarms, and when Foma came up to it and saw them he struck at them and killed a large number. "I am a man of great strength, I am!" said he. "Why should I plough when I can go to war!" And though his neighbours laughed at him and said, "Warring with anyone is not for the likes of you, fool, what you should do is feed the pigs!" it did not stop him. He said that he was a great warrior, one who feared nothing, took an axe and a knife which he used for whittling, put on an old coat and a felt cap, and, getting on his nag, set out from home at an easy pace. And once he was out in the field he drove a pillar into the ground and inscribed it with the following words: "I am off to make war in far-off lands and will smite off a hundred heads at a single blow!"

He rode away, and no sooner had he done so than two mighty warriors

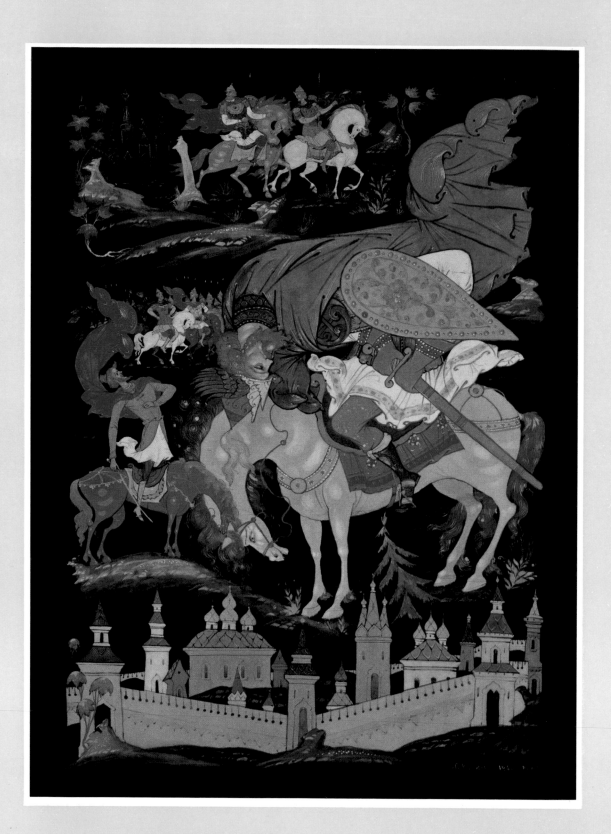

came galloping up to the pillar. They read the inscription and said: "What great warrior is he who wrote that and where is he? There is no sound of giant hoofs and no giant tracks on the ground to tell us where he went." They set out down the road, which happened to be the one Foma was following, and Foma saw them and asked who they were. "Peace to you, good man!" said they. "We are great and mighty warriors." "How many heads can you smite off at one blow?" Foma asked. "Five," said one of the warriors, "Ten," said the other. "Call yourselves mighty warriors!" Foma cried. "Why, you're worthless fellows, both! Now, unlike you, I'm a true warrior, for I can smite off a hundred heads at one blow!" "Then do let us join you," the warriors said. "Very well! Just follow me," said Foma.

And so the three of them set out together for the king's own meadows. They got there soon enough, let their horses wander freely about and lay down for a sleep. Now, whether a short or a long time passed nobody knows, but by and by the king saw them there and said: "Who are those three? Never did a beast prowl in my meadows before, nor a bird fly over them, and now here are those churls fooling away the time there!" And he mustered a numberless host and ordered his meadows cleared of their presence. The host marched upon them, and the two mighty warriors were alarmed and told Foma about it. "Go forth against the host, and I'll see if you are in truth as brave as you said," said Foma.

The two mighty warriors got on their steeds and sent them into a gallop, and they cut down and trampled to death every last one of the warriors. "A sad business this!" said the king, and he mustered another host, twice as big as the first one, and put at its head a giant with a head as large as a cauldron, a brow as large as an oven-door, and a body the size of a mountain. Seeing him, Foma got on his nag and rode out to meet him. "You are a mighty warrior, and I am one too," said he, "and little honour will we have won if we met in combat without greeting each other properly. First must we exchange bows and only then cross swords." "Very well!" said the giant. They drew some distance away from each other and prepared to bow. Now, it took the giant a whole half hour to bend his head, and Foma who, though small, was quick of wits, knew that it would take him another half hour to lift it, so he did not wait for him to do it but struck him with his axe, and the giant's head rolled off his shoulders.

The host scattered, and Foma mounted a giant horse and went after the foes, trampling them as he caught up with them. It could not be helped, and the king owned that he was vanquished. He had his nobles call the mighty warrior Foma Berennikov and his two friends, regaled them with food and drink and bestowed many honours upon them. He then married his daughter to Foma and gave her half his kingdom for a dowry.

Whether a short or a long time passed nobody knows, but a heathen tsar led a great warrior host against Foma's father-in-law, laid siege to his kingdom and demanded a huge tribute of him. The king was loath to give it him, so he mustered a host of his own, put Foma at its head and ordered everyone to watch him and to do as he did.

And Foma did not dally but rode off to fight the enemy. He passed through a forest, and his warriors followed him. He cut down a birch-tree, and his

173

warriors each did the same. They came to a deep river with no bridge across it, and Foma, who knew that the road running round the river was over a hundred miles long, threw his birch-tree into the water. His warriors did the same with theirs, and the river now being dammed, they all crossed easily to the other side. Now, the heathen tsar had entrenched himself firmly in a town, and Foma stopped in a field before it, made up a fire, took off all his clothes and sat there drying himself. His warriors followed suit. They gathered brushwood, chopped up some trees into logs, and made up fires all over the field. "I don't mind if I have a bite!" said Foma, and, taking a flat-cake out of his knapsack, lay to with great appetite. All of a sudden as if out of thin air a dog appeared. It ran up to Foma, snatched the flat-cake out of his hands and made away with it. And Foma grabbed a smouldering brand out of the fire, and, naked as he was, rushed after the dog, shouting at the top of his voice: "Stop it! Seize it!" And his warriors jumped up and each of them grabbing a brand, ran after him.

Now, the dog belonged to the heathen tsar, and it rushed straight through the gate and into the palace. And Foma never stopped but ran after it, with his warriors at his heels. They set fire to whatever came to hand and burnt it down without mercy. The townsfolk were in a panic and so was the tsar who called for a truce. But Foma would not have it. He took the tsar captive and overran and conquered his whole tsardom. And when he came back from the wars his father-in-law met him with great ceremony and bestowed many honours upon him. The music played, the bells rang, the cannon roared, and a great feast was held to celebrate his homecoming. Many were the guests that attended it, and I was among them. *I drank much mead and I drank much wine, and all of it ran down this beard of mine. I had some fowl and I had some game, but my belly stayed empty all the same. They pushed a cap down upon my head, but drove me out, alas, unfed. A lady's bonnet they made me wear, but I scurried away like a frightened hare!* And that is the end of my tale.

Translated by Irina Zheleznova

REQUEST TO READERS

Raduga Publishers would be glad to have your opinion of this book, its translation and design and any suggestions you may have for future publications.

Please send all your commefts to 17, Zubovsky Boulevard, Moscow, USSR.

Перевод сделан по книге:
Народные русские сказки А. Н. Афанасьева.
М., «Советская Россия», 1986.

Для среднего и старшего школьного возраста

Printed in the Union of Soviet Socialist Republics

ИБ № 2638

Редактор русского текста И. Логинов
Контрольные редакторы А. Буяновская, Е. Криштоф
Иллюстрации художника А. Куркина
Оформление художника В. Мирошниченко
Художественный редактор А. Алтунин
Технический редактор А. Агафошина

Сдано в набор 20.01.87. Подписано в печать 01.12.87. Формат
$84 \times 108^1/_{16}$. Бумага мелованная. Гарнитура таймс. Печать
офсет. Условн. печ. л. 18,48. Усл. кр.-отт. 77,48. Уч.-изд.
л. 14,55. Тираж 39 260 экз. Заказ № 896. Цена 3 р. 30 к.
Изд. № 1965

Издательство «Радуга» Государственного комитета СССР
по делам издательств, полиграфии и книжной торговли
Москва, 119859, Зубовский бульвар, 17

Ордена Трудового Красного Знамени Калининский поли-
графический комбинат Союзполиграфпрома при Государ-
ственном комитете СССР по делам издательств, полиграфии и книжной торговли. 170024, г. Калинин, пр. Ленина, 5